THE WIFE-SWAPPERS

THE PROWL • THE BURGLAR WHO COUNTED THE SPOONS • THE BURGLAR IN SHORT ORDER

KELLER'S GREATEST HITS

HIT MAN • HIT LIST • HIT PARADE • HIT & RUN • HIT ME • KELLER'S FEDORA

THE ADVENTURES OF EVAN TANNER

THE THIEF WHO COULDN'T SLEEP • THE CANCELED CZECH • TANNER'S TWELVE SWINGERS • TWO FOR TANNER • TANNER'S TIGER • HERE COMES A HERO • ME TANNER, YOU JANE • TANNER ON ICE

THE AFFAIRS OF CHIP HARRISON

NO SCORE • CHIP HARRISON SCORES AGAIN • MAKE OUT WITH MURDER • THE TOPLESS TULIP CAPER

COLLECTED SHORT STORIES

SOMETIMES THEY BITE • LIKE A LAMB TO SLAUGHTER • SOME DAYS YOU GET THE BEAR • ONE NIGHT STANDS AND LOST WEEKENDS • ENOUGH ROPE • CATCH AND RELEASE • DEFENDER OF THE INNOCENT • RESUME SPEED AND OTHER STORIES

BOOKS FOR WRITERS

WRITING THE NOVEL FROM PLOT TO PRINT TO PIXEL • TELLING LIES FOR FUN & PROFIT • SPIDER, SPIN ME A WEB • WRITE FOR YOUR LIFE • THE LIAR'S BIBLE • THE LIAR'S COMPANION

WRITTEN FOR PERFORMANCE

TILT! (EPISODIC TELEVISION) • HOW FAR? (ONE-ACT PLAY) • MY BLUEBERRY NIGHTS (FILM)

ANTHOLOGIES EDITED

DEATH CRUISE • MASTER'S CHOICE • OPENING SHOTS • MASTER'S CHOICE 2 • SPEAKING OF LUST • OPENING SHOTS 2 • SPEAKING OF GREED • BLOOD ON THEIR HANDS • GANGSTERS, SWINDLERS, KILLERS, & THIEVES • MANHATTAN NOIR • MANHATTAN NOIR 2 • DARK CITY LIGHTS • IN SUNLIGHT OR IN SHADOW • ALIVE IN SHAPE AND COLOR • AT HOME IN THE DARK • FROM SEA TO STORMY SEA • THE DARKLING HALLS OF IVY

21 Gay Street
69 Barrow Street
The Adulterers
April North
Born to be Bad
Campus Tramp
Carla
Circle of Sinners
College for Sinners
Community of Women
Flesh Mob
Flesh Parade
Gigolo Johnny Wells
A Girl Called Honey
Girls on the Prowl
High School Sex Club

I Sell Love
Kept
Lust Weekend
Of Shame and Joy
Passion Nightmare
Sin Bum
The Sin-Damned
Sin Hellcat
Sexpot!
Sintime
A Strange Kind of Love
So Willing
Tramp
The Twisted Ones
The Wife-Swappers
A Woman Must Love

THE WIFE-SWAPPERS
Copyright © 1960, by Lawrence Block
Original Publication, writing as Andrew Shaw

All Rights Reserved. This book or parts thereof may not be reproduced in any form, stored in any retrieval system, or transmitted in any form by any means—spoken, written, photocopy, printed, electronic, mechanical, recording, or otherwise through any means not yet known or in use—without prior written permission of the publisher, except for purposes of review.

Cover & Interior by JW Manus

A LAWRENCE BLOCK PRODUCTION

THE WIFE-SWAPPERS

LAWRENCE BLOCK

Chapter 1

BILL JANSEN RAN A hand over the blonde's behind. It was, he thought absently, a marvelous behind. Trim and neat and well-muscled, but, at the same time, soft and pink and nice to stroke. He held her so that each of his big hands cupped one of her soft buttocks. He squeezed and she giggled pleasantly. He squeezed again, harder, and she let out a moan that was the beginning of passion.

He released her buttocks and let his hands trail gently along her golden legs. She was wearing Bermuda shorts and her thighs were bare. Her skin was the type of skin that tanned easily and exposure to the sun had colored her nicely. Bill could see where the tan began. Above, the thigh swelled and her skin was a succulent pink. He wanted to bite it, to run his lips all over it.

Her name was Linda Pierce. She was short and blonde with a magnificent pair of firm large breasts that went nicely with the thighs and the behind. She drank a little too much and her laughter was brittle, with a vaguely unpleasant edge to it.

This was almost all Bill knew about her. He knew a little bit else, but not much. For one thing, he knew that she had a husband. Her husband was a big florid-faced man with a receding hairline and the slightest suggestion of a paunch. He did something in some incomprehensible area of public relations and earned somewhere between ten and fifteen thousand dollars a year.

His name was Jackson Pierce. He was standing just twelve feet away, a highball in his hand, another woman on his arm. His hand was fondling the other woman's breast.

Bill Jansen touched Linda's thigh. With the fingers of his left hand he raised the material of the Bermuda shorts. The shorts were red plaid and they were expensive, but Bill was more interested in what was going on underneath them. He reached up under the shorts with the fingers of his right hand and stroked the pink skin that the sun hadn't gotten to yet. The skin was soft as silk. And a hell of a lot more fun to touch.

Linda seemed to like it. He sat down and she settled in his lap, her arms curling around him like snakes. Bill got a glimpse of Jackson Pierce out of the corner of his eye. Pierce wasn't paying any attention. He was busy with the woman—his hands were still busy with her breasts and now her hands were playing games of their own, rubbing him and working a visible magic.

Bill took Linda's face between his hands, brought her mouth to his. The kiss was expert—mouths opened, tongues groping. There was no particular urgency in the kiss. It was relaxed, almost dispassionate, the kiss of two able performers letting each other know of their separate abilities. Her tongue was a living being in his mouth and his own tongue welcomed it, embraced it.

He could feel her breasts against his chest. Her blouse was thin and she wasn't wearing a bra. Her breasts were very firm and very warm. He wondered what they would feel like in his big hands.

The kiss ended. She leaned back against his arms and grinned at him. Her eyes were slightly glazed, her lips moist and parted.

"Nice," she said.

"Very nice."

"I could learn to like you."

"You might not be so hard to take yourself. I like the way you're put together."

She giggled. Her giggle was harsh, discordant. "Built for comfort," she said. "Big all over."

"Not here," he said. His hands touched her waist.

"Yeah, but how about here?" Her hands cupped her breasts, holding them like an offering to an idol. He nodded, admitting to her and to himself that they were very large indeed.

"And here," she added. She touched her hips.

He grinned at her. "Not here," he said. "At least I hope not."

She giggled louder than ever. "Hell," she said. "Hell, not there. There I'm tight as a goddamned drum."

He laughed, half with her and half at her, and he began stroking her rear some more.

He wondered if she would be the one he would sleep with that night.

He hoped so. She would be nice and he had never had her before. It would be fun with her, plenty of fun, with her firm breasts under him and her hot mouth pressed to his. It would be plenty of fun.

But it didn't really matter. There were plenty of women there for him.

And they were all damned good.

THE CLUB WAS FOUR months old. Eight couples belonged, eight couples with nothing much in common outside of their mutual residence in the small and eminently respectable suburb of Eastport and their mutual interest in horizontal pleasantries.

The couples ranged in age from Walt and Mary Forsythe, who were pushing forty, to Don and Nedra Marshall, who were pushing twenty-five. Annual income ranged from close to twenty-five thousand in the case of Larry Carson to a little under eight thousand that Bill Jansen earned. Larry Carson was ad manager for Neil and McCowan; Bill Jansen was a junior partner in the middle-bracket law firm of Stults, Litvak and Tauriello.

There were sixteen of them. Walt and Mary Forsythe were the unacknowledged leaders of the club. Walt was tall and lean with a well-muscled body and a look of congenial dissipation much like Errol Flynn. He even had a neat moustache that intensified the impression. His wife was handsome rather than beautiful—good features, rich nut-brown hair, full breasts and plenty of meat on her bones. They made a striking couple, with Walt looking lean and fashionably degenerate while Mary was the classic mother-image. And they had made a good marriage, one that had lasted better than fifteen years. A good amount of tolerance on both sides of the fence eased the strains of marriage that they might otherwise have felt. They knew each other very well, knew and understood each other, and little rifts never seriously damaged their relationship.

Bill and Pidge Jansen were quite different. They were young and they had married after a whirlwind courtship that tossed them into bed as man and wife before they knew very much about each other or about themselves. Pigeon, whose real name was Helena, was a very unstable girl with monumental desires that were balanced by monumental inhibitions. Their marriage slowly but surely headed for the rocks, and they had joined the club for two reasons— to bring some excitement to their lives and to try to save their marriage through alleviation of their overwhelming boredom.

The Marshalls, Don and Nedra, were young marrieds in the full sense of the word. In another environment they would have raised children, joined the PTA, planted flowers in their yard and lived the solid life of solid citizens. Because they lived in Eastport things turned out differently. Both were ready to conform to the societal norm of whatever community they found themselves in. When the societal norm included wife-trading parties, the Marshalls took to the game like ducks to water.

Don Marshall was twenty-four; premature baldness was adding a few years to his appearance. He was tall and rangy with a tendency to slouch and a huge capacity for cold beer. His wife Nedra, whom everybody called Ned, had been a virgin until her wedding night. That night the two of them checked into a motel and Ned found out what she had been missing. Since then she had been making up for lost time with an incredible ability.

Jackson Pierce, whose wife had been carrying on such a pleasant series of games with Bill Jansen, was in the process of becoming an alcoholic. He was in the unhappy position of the college football star who had been a hero in his undergraduate days and who had since discovered that he wasn't much good for anything other than smashing off a tackle or running the ends. His reputation at Princeton had secured him a nice berth in a good public relations firm—a lot of clients were easily impressed by ex-athletes and that was what earned him his salary.

As he got older he became progressively less valuable, both to the firm and to himself. His wife Linda was an intellectual type, a book-reader, a phrase-spouter. Every day they seemed to have less in common. The club gave them an out; a way to remain married without remaining quite so bored with each other. And, while he waited for his own private Armageddon, Jackson Pierce calmly and quietly worked on the task of drinking himself to death.

Sue and Larry Carson were easily the most striking couple physically. Larry had catapulted to the head advertising slot at Neil and McCowan not by playing the organization game as a good team man but by earning a reputation for brilliant eccentricity. He had a neatly trimmed red beard, a long face and piercing brown eyes. He talked quickly and forcefully, slipping at will from penetrating analysis to flip humor and back again. His wife Sue had long light brown hair that she wore hanging free to her waist. Like her husband she had an insatiable appetite for the unusual. This interest in experimentation rather than marital unhappiness was responsible for the presence of the Carsons in the club.

There were three more couples. Steve and Nancy Gordon, Mark and Peggy Phillips, Joe and Roz Robshaw. They were all between twenty-five and thirty, all somehow connected with the advertising-public relations-television octopus, all young and confused and hungry for something new and different. And all members of the club.

The club had no name, no official identity. Meetings were held once every two weeks on alternate Saturdays at the home of one of the member couples. The meetings themselves were relatively routine, just typical suburban parties with a good deal to drink, good jazz on the hi-fi, flip conversation and cool camaraderie.

At first a spectator might see no difference whatsoever between a meeting of the nameless club and any suburban weekend get-together. But a closer look revealed a few not-too-subtle distinctions.

In any group of married couples it is not uncommon for men to kiss other men's wives. But at the meetings of the club these kisses were deeper, longer, more insistent. The casual banter was not so casual and the caresses that accompanied the kisses were downright sexual.

It would not be cause for remark at any party if Bill Jansen were to grab Linda Pierce and give her a kiss. But at the average party he wouldn't stroke her behind and run his hands up her thighs.

It would be quite normal for Jackson Pierce to drop an arm around Nancy Gordon. It would not be normal for him to cup her breast and give it a squeeze. Nor would it be normal for her to moan softly and rub her rear against him like a kitten in heat.

There was one rule at the parties, one rule and one rule alone. Petting could go as far as it wanted, but no one was permitted to engage in intercourse during the course of the party.

That came later.

Later, when the women retired to another room and tossed their house keys into a hat. Later, when the men picked the women's keys from the hat to find out who would be sleeping with whom. Then the party was over. Then the newly-formed couples would retire to the home of the woman and do whatever they pleased.

They only saw each other once every two weeks. No affairs were carried on, no outside alliances were allowed to disturb the individual marriages. Each husband remained true to his wife for thirteen days out of every fourteen. Then the club met and the tensions were released with another man's wife in another man's bed.

It was a good arrangement, very modern, very suburban, very twentieth-century. Monogamy was no longer synonymous with monotony. Men and women had the opportunity to sample fresh flesh before they returned to their lawful mates.

It worked very well.

And if some women cried in the night because guilt rode on their shoulders like the albatross on the shoulders of the ancient mariner, this was just part of the game. And if some men shook with the fear that another man would get their wives pregnant, this too was part of the game.

The club was an entity unto itself. It lived and breathed. Every other Saturday was meeting night, take-it-easy night, let-out-your-tensions night, everything-goes night.

So let's get back to the party. This particular meeting, the fourth since the formation of the club is taking place at the home of Joe and Roz Robshaw. The Robshaws live on

Tareyton Road in a small brick-front house. They have no children.

Roz Robshaw is in the kitchen preparing a tray of hors d'oeuvres. She is not alone. Walt Forsythe is with her, one hand up under her full skirt, clutching her, the other hand on her buttocks holding her close. Their bodies are close together, their mouths meet in a long and passionate kiss. Roz is wondering what it would be like with Walt. He's so debonair, so suave, so sure of himself. That's what she's always missed in Joe. Oh, Joe's a fine man, a good man, the only man she could possibly be happy being married to. He makes good money and loves her and takes good care of her. But something's missing, and she thinks that perhaps Walt will supply it.

Walt, on his part, wants Roz. She's a fine figure of a woman, big in the breasts, wide in the hips. And she's hot as a two-dollar pistol. He can tell. He thinks of a few things he'd like to do to her and his blood races.

Nedra Marshall comes in to get a drink of water. She sees Walt and Roz and grins. They end their kiss and she walks to them and puts an arm around both of them.

"Got a kiss for me, Walt?"

She and Walt made love two weeks ago. She is still tingling from the memory of it.

He kisses her, then pinches her in a very pinchable place. She giggles and pulls away.

"What time is it, Walt?"

"Almost midnight."

"Then it's time."

"Just about."

"I'll call the girls."

Roz Robshaw goes into the living room. As hostess it's her job to let the women know when to throw their keys in the hat. She walks from one girl to the next holding out an old hat of Joe's to receive the keys. Each woman in turn drops her housekey into the hat. To simplify things, each key has its owner's initials scratched on the back of it.

Automatically all the men and women form a semicircle in the living room. Roz stands in the middle, the hat held in both hands. She shakes it and the keys jingle like a sack full of coins.

Anticipation shines in each pair of eyes. Faces are flushed, bodies tense. There is a savage look in the eyes of some of the women, an insanely hungry look in the eyes of some of the men. Here and there a calm man or woman stands, eyes empty, face expressionless. But most of them are obviously highly-keyed, tense, excited.

"Off we go," Roz says. She shakes the hat, tosses the keys a few inches into the air and catches them in the hat. Her smile widens.

"You're first, Larry."

LARRY CARSON WAS FIRST. He walked to the hat, a gentle smile on his face. He reached in, took out a key and studied it.

"N.G.," he read. "That must be you, Nancy."

He walked to Nancy Gordon and took her arm. They hadn't been together before and both were obviously pleased by the arrangement. She cuddled close to him and he kissed her briefly on the mouth.

They walked to the door. Her husband Steve told Larry to take good care of her. He laughed and they went out through the door and into his car, a cream-colored Lincoln. He kissed her, ran his hands over her body, then fitted the key in the ignition and started the car. The big Lincoln purred kittenishly and pulled away from the curb.

Don Marshall was next. The key he drew was initialed MF and belonged to Mary Forsythe. This drew a few laughs since Mary was a good twelve years older than he was. But neither of them seemed to mind the disparity in their ages. They hurried out of the house as if they couldn't wait to get into bed.

Walt Forsythe drew next, picking Pidge Jansen. He didn't recognize the key at first—it was initialed HJ and it took a minute before he remembered that her name was Helena. Walt and Pidge both seemed pleased but Roz Robshaw was disappointed. She'd hoped for a chance with Walt, and now she wondered who she would wind up with.

Walt and Pidge left and the tension in the room was almost audible now. There were five couples left, all of them highly strung by now, all of them anxious to pair off and get down to serious business. It was Jackson Pierce's turn to draw and he prolonged the agony by taking a long time to pick a key.

When he did pick one he read the initials solemnly and discovered that he had drawn his own wife's key. He laughed, easing the tension momentarily, and flipped the key back into the hat.

Roz shook the keys around. Pierce wavered drunkenly, then reached in again. He pulled out the key and stared at it unbelievingly.

"I'll be a son of a bitch," he said. "I did it again. That's a hell of a note."

"Careful," somebody called. "If you pick her three times you've got to keep her."

"What the hell," Pierce said. "It's not as though she's a bad piece."

Roz Robshaw swirled the keys around in the hat. Jackson Pierce reached in, pulled out a key.

"RR," he said. "That's you, honey." And he reached for Roz and squeezed her breast.

"You'll have to wait," she said. "Until all the others are gone."

Pierce nodded. He and Roz had been together the first week and the results had been embarrassing. Too much to drink had made him unequal to the task with which he had been confronted. It was simply a biological impossibility and the two of them went almost insane. Roz had been crawling the walls until finally he had made love to her in a manner which satisfied her without requiring any expenditure of energy on his part.

But this time, he told himself, it would be different. He wasn't that drunk this time and he'd take care of her. He'd give her the time of her life.

Four more to go. Bill Jansen got Linda Pierce on the first draw and the two of them left the house with stars in their eyes. The necking session they'd gone through earlier in the evening hadn't left them exactly relaxed and they almost got down to brass tacks in the car instead of waiting until they got to Linda's house. As it was, Bill could barely drive. Linda was squirming all over him, her hands exciting him past the point of anything approaching calmness. When he reached her house they raced up the steps, their hearts pounding like triphammers.

Three left. Mark Phillips, a very intense young man who said very little to anybody, drew his wife once, then picked Sue Carson's key. He gripped her arm very tightly and there was a strange and frightening light gleaming in his dark eyes.

They left without saying a word.

Steve Gordon drew Mark's wife, Peggy Phillips. And away they went.

That left Joe Robshaw with Nedra Marshall. By this time, the suspense had become unbearable. Standing around, trying to be calm, thinking of what the others were doing, thinking of sweating bodies and heaving hearts, thinking of lust and passion, was hardly the way to remain calm.

Joe Robshaw and Ned Marshall were not calm. They were anything but calm. Joe felt like throwing her down on the rug and having her then and there.

Nedra felt like letting him.

But they had to play the game according to the rules. And the rules stated simply that nothing was to happen outside of the bed of the woman involved. Joe and Ned left. Joe backed his car out of the driveway and Ned hopped into the front seat next to him. They kissed once and their passion simply soared that much higher.

He drove very fast to her house.

Jackson Pierce and Roz Robshaw were left. The house was empty and the living room was a mess with the residue of the party. Empty glasses made rings on tables and beer cans cluttered the carpet that ran wall-to-wall in the large room.

The house had a weird feel to it, the feel that follows a party. It was as if the guests were still there in spirit, as if some part of them remained to haunt the room. Pierce looked at Roz and Roz looked back at him. They were both very conscious of each other and very conscious of the room. For a long time neither of them said a word.

Then Pierce broke the silence. "I'm sorry about last time, Roz."

"It wasn't your fault."

"It was. I shouldn't have hit the bottle so hard. I drink enough during the week. I can afford to take it easy when it matters."

She smiled gently. She was a gentle woman, a warm woman. "It's okay," she said. "It was bad at first but I enjoyed myself enough later on."

He grinned, remembering what they had done and the way she had reacted.

"You did all right," he admitted. "But I didn't. I was too stoned to get much out of it. And I want to get all I can when I'm with a woman like you. You're a hell of a lot of woman, Roz."

"You think so?"

He nodded solemnly.

"Your wife's not bad herself."

He shrugged. "A nice girl," he said. "But not a woman. A sweet little bit of fluff with nice boobs and a nice behind. Not a woman, Roz. A girl. A little girl who married me because I was a big important football player with a nice house and a pile of money. That's all. She hasn't got any real warmth to her, except between those thighs of hers. And that's not enough. That part of it wears off after awhile. You get used to passion. It's almost . . . well, dull, after a certain amount of time."

"Honestly?"

"Honestly. There's a sameness to it that's pretty damned boring. You know, it's funny. Linda's the intellect in the family and I'm the athletic lush. But she's so shallow that it ought to be the other way around. I could use a little more depth."

"Is your marriage going?"

"No, we'll stick it out. At the bottom we're good for each other. Neither of us could live with anybody else without going crazy. I suppose we're in love, if you want to call it that. But I need a change."

She looked at him and suddenly it was as though she was seeing him for the first time. She was very glad that they were going to be together tonight, very glad. The disappointment of missing a chance with Walt Forsythe had faded and disappeared now. She was seeing a new side of Jackson and she wanted a chance to know him, to know him completely, to get a glimpse of him that could only be gained through wholehearted lovemaking, to share an experience with him, to know him the way a woman knows a lover.

"Let's go upstairs."

He nodded. He walked to her slowly and took her in his arms. She melted against him and she was aware of his body against her, aware of the feel of him, aware of him and in need of him.

He took her arm and led her to the staircase. They climbed the stairs slowly, their need a gradual thing rather than a hot and quick and demanding passion. They climbed the stairs with their minds groping out, their personalities opening up to one another.

They didn't talk. It wasn't necessary. At the head of the stairs she turned to face him and their mouths met in a long kiss.

They walked to the bedroom. Inside with the door shut they turned away from one another like virgin newlyweds, shy all at once, vaguely embarrassed. They undressed, then turned once again and looked at one another.

"You're lovely, Roz."

"Do you think so?"

"Yes."

They lay down on the bed and he began to kiss her. He kissed her mouth and her throat and her breasts. Her breasts were large and soft and warm, and when he kissed them the nipples stiffened and became unbearably sensitive.

"Slowly, Jackson."

He went slowly. He made it last a long time, a very long time, and it was good from beginning to end. It started slowly and gently and built to an overwhelming crescendo of feeling and emotion. They moved higher and higher until they reached the crest of passion. The wave broke simultaneously for both of them and they went limp and flaccid, their bodies streaked with sweat, their hearts pounding like jungle drums in a bad movie.

"That was good," she said.

He said her name and nothing more.

They slept.

MARK PHILLIPS DIDN'T TALK much. He was an accountant, a silent and solitary profession, and he was at his best when he played with numbers. He could do wild and wonderful things with numbers. He could save people quite a bit of money at tax time, and as a result he was well paid.

He was not a very nice man.

He was with Sue Carson now in the house Sue and Larry shared. It was a very large and very expensive house on Mamaroneck Parkway. They were in the master bedroom. Chad Carson, Larry and Sue's three-year-old son, slept peacefully down the hall.

Mark and Sue were naked. They were sitting side by side on the bed, staring across the room at the bureau. They said nothing for a long time.

"I'm glad I got you," he said. "I know a lot about you. Things nobody else knows."

She looked at him, frightened.

"I know what your kick is," he went on. "You like pain. You like to get hurt."

"How did you know?"

"I can see it in your eyes. It's true, isn't it?"

She nodded, ashamed.

"It's nothing to hide. It's your particular kick. You've got a right to it."

"But it's—"

"What?"

"—perverted."

He laughed. It was not a pleasant laugh. By no stretch of the imagination could it be called a pleasant laugh.

"Don't say perverted," he said. "Say different."

She didn't say anything. He reached for her, grabbed her breast and squeezed. His hands were wiry and his grip was strong. He hurt her.

She moaned.

"You like it, don't you?"

She nodded, blushing with shame.

"Roll over," he told her. "Lie on your stomach for awhile."

"Why?"

"Because I'm going to spank you."

"Please—"

"Do what I say!"

She rolled over. He straddled her and began to rain blows on her posterior, slapping with his open palm. At first the slaps were light but gradually they increased in intensity until he was hitting her as hard as he could.

She moaned. Half in pain. Half in pleasure.

"Mark—"

"Shut up!"

He slapped her some more, harder. She began to writhe now, squirming on the bed.

"Roll over."

She rolled over onto her back, her body glistening with sweat. "Now," she begged him. "Don't make me wait any longer. I'm ready, Mark. Do it to me. You know what I want. Do it to me!"

His reply was a slap. He hit her breast and she screamed.

Her breasts were large and extraordinarily tender and the pain was like a knife in her side.

He hit her again.

Harder.

"God, Mark! Not any more. Do it, Mark. Do it to me. I can't wait any longer."

But he made her wait. He kept beating her until he couldn't wait any more either, beat her as hard as he could until his passion was equal to hers.

Then he took her, hungrily, greedily, painfully, took her and used her cruelly while her screams wailed in his ears.

Chapter 2

"LARRY?"

A grunt.

"Larry, wake up."

The bearded advertising manager rolled over onto his side. He grunted again, then rubbed a hand over his eyes. His eyes opened.

"It's almost five, Larry."

"Sleeping."

"It's almost five. Steve'll be home any minute. It's time for you to go home."

A yawn.

"Come on, Larry. Please?"

Carson sat up on the edge of the bed. He yawned again, then grinned. He reached over and cupped one of Nancy Gordon's breasts in his hand.

"Nice stuff, Nance."

"Larry—"

"You're okay, Nance. Thanks for a very pleasant evening. You sure know what you're doing in the hay. I guess Steve has no cause for complaints."

"Neither does Sue."

He went on stroking her breasts. The gesture now was sexless. It was the friendly caress of two people who have been extremely intimate and who are consequently able to relax with one another.

"Wonder who Sue wound up with tonight."

"I don't know. I wonder whose bed Steve's in."

"Maybe they wound up together."

Nancy Gordon grinned. "That would be funny," she said. "I don't know. I'd feel funny about that. I mean, you and I doing it while my husband was doing it with your wife. It would be strange."

"I suppose so."

He stood up, reached around for his clothing. While he dressed she watched him from the bed, looking at him, remembering what they had done together. Her cheeks flushed, partly from the memory, partly from some hidden well of shame and embarrassment.

When he was dressed he came back and sat down beside her. He touched her breasts again and grinned.

"Nice," he said again. "We'll have to do this some more."

She looked at him, her eyes vaguely troubled. Then she seemed to relax, taking his hand with hers and pressing it tight against her breast.

"You'd better go now," she said.

He smiled. Then he stood up and walked out of the bedroom, down the stairs and out of the house to his car. As he drove off the smile on his face widened slightly when he heard Steve Gordon's car approaching the house from the other direction.

He stepped down hard on the accelerator and the sleek Lincoln shot forward, taking him home, to his wife.

BILL JANSEN HAD NOT slept at all. He was tired now, too tired to move. He saw the sun coming up in the east and the light of it hurt his eyes. But he barely had the strength to close them.

He felt Linda's hands on his body—small hands, deft hands. She touched his back, his thighs. Her hands seemed to know just what to do.

He was tired, terribly tired. How many times had they made love? He didn't remember, didn't have the strength to keep score. God, the girl wasn't human. It would take an army to satisfy her. She just wanted more and more and more. She never got enough.

Now he was about as interested in lovemaking as he was in disemboweling himself. But that wasn't going to stop her. Not at all. Her hands were still doing their dirty work with commendable efficiency. He didn't want to respond but she was just too dammed good at what she was doing. He felt himself responding in spite of himself, felt the beginnings of desire in his exhausted body.

Gently but forcefully she rolled him over onto his back and let herself down on top of him. She took the active role now while he simply lay there. He felt as though he was being raped.

It didn't last very long. Then it was over and he was totally and completely drained. A shadow of contentment passed over her pretty face and her two proud breasts rose and fell with her ragged breathing.

"Like that?"

He managed a nod.

"This was fun," she said. "God, I needed this. Every bit of it."

"You sure you got enough?"

She pouted. "Don't be nasty."

"I'm sorry."

"I'm not a nymphomaniac, if that's what you mean. I just like men. I have what they call a very short fuse. Just a kiss or a touch sets me off and I can't hold myself back. I need all I can get when that happens."

"Just from a kiss?"

She nodded. "Sometimes just from thinking about it. I'll be lying in bed next to Jackson and I'll get to thinking about it and I know he's too tired but I can't help it. It's either get him to make love to me or start climbing the walls. I can't help it."

"You'll kill him, you know."

"It used to be worse, Bill. When I get used to a man it's easier for me. This was the first time I did it with you and that's why I got so wild. I'm sorry."

"Don't apologize. To tell you the truth, I kind of liked it."

She didn't say anything. He looked at her and he saw something strange in her eyes. When she spoke her voice was thin, taut, brittle.

"It's late, Bill. You better go home to Pigeon."

"Okay."

"Hurry up. I'm starting to want you again. If you get out of here I'll be all right."

He got up and began dressing. She rolled over, burying her face in the pillow, and he hurried into his clothing and left the house.

IN EIGHT EASTPORT HOMES eight husbands came home to their wives. It is traditional in Suburbia for the good wife to meet her husband with a shaker of dry martinis when he comes home from a hard day at the office. But it was different with these eight particular Eastport couples. These eight husbands came home on a Sunday morning, and their eight wives did not meet them at the door. They were waiting in bed, soft and warm and sated, smelling of other men.

It was a good morning—warm, sunny, the air clear and the ground smelling of new grass. Soon the crabgrass would start its periodic assault upon each and every Eastport lawn, but this early in the year the lawns were uniformly fresh and green.

Eight husbands came home to eight wives. These eight husbands undressed and joined their wives in bed. Eight couples slept. Later in the day they would wake up, eat Sunday breakfast, lounge around the house reading the massive Sunday edition of the *New York Times*. It would be a quiet day, climaxed probably by dinner at a medium-priced local restaurant, then a few hours of television watching, then an early trip to bed so that the men would be well rested when they went to the office the following morning.

The Good Life. The Normal Patterned Middle-Class American Way of Life. Work from nine to five Monday through Friday. Marriage and a family. A good home, a television set with a big screen, a hi-fi system, a late-model car, preferably two. A way of life that can most be characterized by the very stylized nature of it, with even leisure time apportioned quite meticulously.

The astounding fact, buried in the middle of all this order, is that these eight couples are members of a club that is in marked contravention of all the established rules of order, a club where the members trade wives once every two weeks and copulate like hopped-up rabbits.

In quite another context a gentleman observed: "The horror, gentlemen, is that there is no horror." And it fits here. Eight couples trade wives, eight couples make adultery the high point of their social lives, and these eight couples accept this as part of the standard state of affairs.

If you asked these couples they would tell you that their wife-swapping, or mate-switching, or sex-clubbing, was a practice with a considerable number of advantages and nothing whatsoever on the minus side of the scale. They would talk knowingly of variety, of true marriage devoid of sexual bondage, of a much finer marital union resulting from their periodic infidelities.

They would be lying. Consciously or unconsciously they would be leaving out part of the picture. Whether or not they were aware of the deception, they would be failing to present things as they really are.

Take Sue Carson, for example. She and Larry have what anybody, themselves included, would call an ideal marriage. But after this particular Saturday evening Sue is troubled, very troubled. She doesn't let Larry know of the trouble that haunts her.

But it is there just the same.

Mark Phillips taught her something. Brutally, savagely, he forced her to face something which she had quite successfully buried within herself up to this point. He was a man who liked to inflict pain; she was a woman who enjoyed being hurt. She knew this now and she could not forget it.

Her breasts ached from the beatings he had given her. Her whole body ached in a variety of interesting places. There was a cigarette burn high on the inside of her white thigh that would hurt for a long time. Every time she felt the pain of it she would remember the insane light in his eyes when he had held the end of the cigarette against her flesh and listened to her agonized moans.

Moreover, she would remember how she had liked it, liked the pain that shot through her.

It was not a nice thing to remember.

Or take Roz Robshaw, who had found a degree of empathy with Jackson Pierce which ran much deeper than any experience she had shared with her husband Joe. Previously her affairs within the club were variety; pleasant in and of themselves but no more far-reaching than one-night stands.

This was different.

She hadn't wanted Jackson to leave that morning. It wasn't sex, although the sex they had shared had been very good and very satisfying. It was a mutual understanding which terrified her. She didn't love Jackson; love in any form had nothing to do with it. But she understood him and he understood her in a way that was infinitely more profound than the understanding that was the basis of her marriage.

And she was worried.

Not worried that anything would develop between her and Jackson. Nothing would. Her worry took a different form entirely.

She was worried because she knew that her marriage was going to seem progressively less satisfying. She and Joe had been happy, but their empty happiness would become less and less significant now that she knew what kind of relationship two human beings were capable of. In time their marriage might rot. It would end either in divorce or in the frigid monotony of two people who remain married but who do not remain in love with each other.

These were two examples. Other tensions had been

building up for several weeks, others were beginning to grow, still others would emerge in the weeks ahead. Human beings are weak at best. Twentieth-century society is tension-wrought and insecure in its most placid form. When people push themselves too far and draw their souls out too thin something must snap.

Watch.

IT WAS TUESDAY AFTERNOON. Tuesday afternoon was not pleasant at all. The sun had abandoned it and the day which had started off cold and gray had become cold and gray and wet. The rain had come, an off-again on-again rain that was never entirely absent and that never had the guts to come down in torrents. It was mild enough so that it could fake a person into going out on the street without a hat or umbrella and strong enough so that it could soak a person to the skin.

In Eastport, the rain is not so bad. It soaks into the lawns and makes them greener. It's a clean rain and it clears the air.

In New York, the rain is horrible. The New York air is always filthy and dust-filled and the rain that falls through it picks up the dust and stinks of it. Instead of soaking into lawns it runs along the pavement in foul little rivers.

Walter Forsythe was escaping the New York rain in a bar. The name of the bar was Limbo Inn. It was clean and cool and the drinks were expensive. Around the corner there was an office building, and on the twenty-second floor of this office building there was an office where Walter For-sythe worked.

But Walt wasn't working now. He was sitting in a booth by himself, drinking bourbon sours and thinking. He should have been working, but fortunately Walt Forsythe was important enough so that he could knock off a while whenever he felt like it. Which was fortunate, because he certainly didn't feel like working. He felt like sitting in Limbo Inn and drinking bourbon sours.

He was thinking about the club. Things were proceeding nicely, he had to admit. He remembered the warm and very young body of Pidge Jansen and a warmth spread through him, a warmth that the bourbon sours helped along. She had been sweet and simple, and although she had hardly known many of the fine points of the game of love, she was a willing pupil and a quick study.

He remembered the other women, wives of other members, and then he let his mind relax and remembered some of the other women who had made his life easier to bear. The first one, years and years ago. The others after her.

Women made life almost worthwhile.

The club was going nicely. The original fear and reluctance of the others had been eroded almost entirely by time and experience. A lesser man than Walt Forsythe might well have been content with things as they were.

Walt was not content.

He sipped his drink, then set it down on the marble-topped table and took a cigarette case from his inside jacket pocket. He fitted one of the cigarettes into a short ebony holder and lit it with a silver lighter. He alternately smoked the cigarette and sipped the bourbon sour. They blended nicely. He finished them at about the same time and motioned for another drink.

The trouble was, things never were quite the way he wanted them. There was no denying the progress he was making. But what he had in mind was a good deal more exotic than a simple swapping arrangement.

He closed his eyes and pictured things as he wished them to be. A cult, a genuine cult worshipping the mad evil goddess of sex. A club where the niceties of lust were overwhelmed by the twisted hungers of the flesh. A club where everything went, everything possible, everything that anybody could imagine.

One by one he pictured the eight female members in his mind. His own wife first; of course. But there were few surprises left for him with Mary. She was his wife, his woman, and the similarities of their appetites would keep them united forever. She was the only woman who could match him, the only one whose passion was equal to his own.

He thought about the others. Nedra Marshall, so young, so fresh, so eager and exciting. Sut Carson, so calm and secure on the surface, but with such a warped soul inside. Linda Pierce, vibrant and alive with a tendency toward hysteria bubbling beneath the exterior, hungry, insatiable.

Pidge Jansen, the most recent conquest, a very neurotic girl racing for an inevitable crack up. Peggy Phillips, a lesbian married to a sadist. He wondered idly whether Peggy knew that she was homosexual, whether any experiences in high school or college had let her latent tendencies out into the open. It would be fun to watch those tendencies come into the forefront, to see how the others reacted to them. Great fun. And very interesting.

Nancy Gordon and Roz Robshaw. Normal girls, theoretically. A lot saner and safer than the others. But if they stuck with the group and if the group developed as Walt wanted it to develop, that normality of theirs would have a few strains on it. They'd either get out while they had the chance or go under with the rest. He hoped they'd stay aboard for the ride. It would be fun to watch the normal ones crack apart, to see the unknown flaws inside them emerge from the wreckage.

His mind raced ahead. The next meeting was in two weeks at his house. That gave him a chance to set the stage properly. So far the parties themselves had been innocent fun—kisses, caresses, nothing more. The actual physical sex had been reserved and private.

That would have to change.

He could play games with the liquor, of course. Certain compounds, subtle aphrodisiacs, could bring out qualities that would otherwise stay hidden. Not the elementary stuff like Spanish Fly, but compounds like ginseng and wolfbane that had a more psychological effect.

But that was cheating. It was easy, but the particular personality of Walter Forsythe wanted something more elaborate. It was infinitely more satisfying to watch people destroy themselves than to do all the destruction for them.

He remembered a sweet little redhead, seventeen years old, who slashed both her wrists with a razor blade and had subsequently bled to death in a furnished room in Greenwich Village just ten years ago. When he had met her she had been a virgin, young, totally unversed in anything sensual. But the seeds of self-destruction had been present and he had been able to recognize them. He worked on them, developed them. The girl lived a full life in two short months before she saw her image in some personal mirror and opened her veins to eternity.

Memories.

No drugs, no chemicals. A movie first—that would liven things up. The right movie and the right mood music, something soft and sensuous, musical colors rising and falling in a sensuous sea of sound.

That would be the starter.

He finished his drink and put a ten dollar bill on the table to cover the drinks and tip. On the way back to his office his step was light and easy. He had a plan now, a method of operations.

He didn't even notice the rain.

PEGGY PHILLIPS WAS ALL alone in the house. And she was damned glad of it.

Mark was out bowling with some of his friends. He always bowled on Thursday nights. Jimmy was at a Cub Scout meeting, which was also normal for Thursday night. And Kathy was over at Sandy Nelson's house for a combination or homework and girl-talk.

And she wished they'd stay away as long as they possibly could.

It wasn't as though she didn't love her husband. She loved Mark, for God's sake. He was a strange man and he kept a lot of himself hidden, but she loved him.

And she certainly loved the kids. It was just that she couldn't stand having them around.

She shook her head. That was a hell of a way for a mother to think, but she couldn't help it. She loved them, they were her babies, her children. But they were such a damn pain in the neck, yelling, whining, wanting this and that and God only knew what else.

It was better being alone.

But it wasn't so wonderful being alone either. Whether she was alone or with her family the same nagging pain in the back of her head was always present, a little twitching ache not unlike a tight wire being plucked very sharply and twanging back and forth.

It was that damned club.

The club that she enjoyed and hated at once. The club that excited her and sickened her until she was pulled in two directions so hard she feared she was going to snap in two, to break apart into two separate people.

It was all Mark's idea. When he mentioned it to her the first time she had laughed, thinking it was another of his crazy jokes. Then when he kept harping on the subject she realized that he was serious, that he wasn't kidding at all.

So she fought. She told him it was a horrible idea, a fine thing for sick depraved people but not her type of fun at all. She argued all right. But arguing with Mark was like pushing at the rock of Gibraltar. It didn't do a bit of good.

And, in the end, he had won. They joined the club and went to the parties, and after them she slept with whatever man drew her key from whatever hat the keys had been collected in. Sometimes it was good and sometimes it was not so good. Sometimes her body sang with excitement and her responses were real and true; other times she didn't feel a thing and had to feign passion.

But that was all right. Even with Mark, she didn't always enjoy sex. No, it wasn't the sex itself that bothered her.

It was the parties themselves.

She would sit with a man and watch the others, watch a man running his hot hands over a woman's body. And she would think thoughts that she thought she was through with forever.

Thoughts about women.

Bad thoughts.

Now she was thinking about the time in college. The girl's name had been Andrea Tompkins. Andy for short. The girl had been big and beautiful and large-breasted, all the things that Peggy herself was not. The girl had been intelligent and sophisticated, two other things that Peggy was not.

The girl had also been a lesbian.

It had only happened three times. Once when Peggy was a little drunk and didn't realize exactly what was going on. Not much did go on, not the first time. Andy's mouth kissing her, Andy's hands touching her, Andy's breasts tight against her own breasts.

The other two times were different.

Because there she did know what was going on. And she let it happen. And she enjoyed it.

They were naked those two times. Naked and in bed with a sheet over them to protect them from the world. Andy's hot mouth had been everywhere, kissing, licking, working devilishly on her breasts and belly and thighs until she thought she would go stark raving mad, with everything getting better and more delicious until the whole world exploded into smithereens, shooting into the stratosphere in an orgy of sensation.

Just twice.

Then Andy was gone, expelled for being caught with another girl. And Peggy had stopped and taken a long look at herself and realized what she was becoming. A lesbian. Sick. Twisted. Abnormal.

It would have been very easy for her to go on that way. Too easy. All she had to do was give in to herself, search for another girl interested in the same sort of thing and let a relationship develop naturally. If there had been a girl around like Andy, that might very well have been what happened. But if there was such a girl on campus Peggy didn't know her.

So she fought. She wasn't the type of lesbian who was incapable of enjoying heterosexual relations. She was what the books she read called bisexual, and she worked very hard to let the heterosexual side of her personality develop. She went a bit farther with the boys she dated than she otherwise would have gone, until suddenly she wasn't a virgin any more.

From there on it was easy. Men took the place of women. Sex became a man-woman thing. There weren't that many men, she was never really promiscuous, and in her junior year of college there was Mark and marriage.

And children.

Now she was a suburban housewife, a woman with a home and a family. Whatever lesbian desires remained came only in dreams that she forgot by the time she woke up. Andy was a hazy memory, a vague recollection of another lifetime in another world.

Now she was afraid.

The club was doing it, the filthy horrible rotten stinking club. She would go to their meetings and watch what the men did to the women, watch hands on breasts and buttocks. The desire the women felt was a living force—

she could sit in another man's arms and feel the heat of the women permeating the room.

It was too much.

Then the pairing-off, the hide-the-keys nonsense, the climax of the party which was to her an anticlimax. She would go home with a man, any man, using the man to sate the desire awakened by the women.

I'm not a lesbian, she told herself. I had one little affair in college before I was old enough to know what the hell I was doing. I had it and I liked it but that doesn't mean a thing. Anybody would like it.

God!

She took a deep breath and let it out slowly. Things had been all right for awhile. She had settled down, purged the old memories and stifled the old desires. But now they were coming back. Now she could remember, for instance, just how it had felt when she had taken the nipple of Andy's big breast between her lips, how nice it had been to kiss those breasts while Andy squirmed and moaned in rich and genuine passion.

God above!

And Mary Forsythe reminded her of Andy. That was the horrible thing, the thing she couldn't even bear to think about.

Mary Forsythe looked like Andy. A big woman, a woman with huge breasts and wide hips. A woman she couldn't watch without feeling the fires start to glow and smolder between her own warm thighs.

Saturday night it had been Don Marshall's turn to go off with Mary Forsythe. It was a laughable thought—she was at least ten years older than he was. It was almost obscene; the thought of Don and Mary together. *Almost* obscene—that was a hell of a way to describe it.

But it was worse when she paired off with Steve Gordon. Because when she lay there in her bed, with Steve making love to her, all she could think of was Mary, Mary, Mary. She closed her eyes and tried to pretend that Steve was not Steve at all, not a man at all, that it was Mary with her and Mary who was doing those things to her.

God in heaven!

She threw herself into a chair, fighting with herself, fighting to be calm. It would be all right. Everything would be all right.

She would work it out.

But how?

How?

Methodically she forced herself to walk to the living room, to take a pack of playing cards from the buffet and to sit down at the card table and deal out a game of solitaire. Sometimes she could lose herself in solitaire. Sometimes moving the cards around could get her mind away from the bad things that she didn't want to think about.

Sometimes.

It didn't work at first. At first she dealt out the cards and moved red queens onto black kings and black jacks onto red queens without even thinking about what she was doing.

Instead she thought of Mary, and because she did not want to think of Mary her headache got worse and worse with the little wire in the back of her skull vibrating faster and faster until she was sure her head would crack down the middle.

She kept on playing. And, gradually, she relaxed. Not entirely—there was still the headache, still the dull pit of shame and fear, still the agony and the worry and the anxiety and all the rest. But the cards worked their subtle magic and the worst of it was over.

She played many games. She played until first Kathy and then Jimmy and finally Mark came home. She listened to the stupid stories the kids told her, listened when Mark bragged about his bowling, listened to all these things without actually hearing anything but disconnected words and phrases.

Then the kids were off to bed and Mark came to her. He wanted to make love and she thought that they ought to make love, that maybe that would get the other thoughts out of her mind, at least for the time being.

But she did not want to make love.

That was all there was to it.

She told him that she had a headache. He argued a while, then dropped it. She took a couple aspirin and got into bed; a few minutes later he joined her and fell asleep at once.

Not her.

She lay there, alone and afraid, until sleep came many hours later.

Chapter 3

JOE ROBSHAW WAS READING the paper. At least he was trying to read the paper. Somehow it didn't seem to be working out properly. It wasn't working at all, as a matter of fact, because he kept finding himself reading the second paragraph of an article without remembering what the first paragraph had had to say. This wasn't the best way in the world to read the paper. It wasn't the best way in the world to do much of anything, when you came right down to it.

It wasn't as though the paper was dull. Joe was reading the financial pages and the financial pages were the most interesting part of the paper as far as he was concerned. He worked at a brokerage house on Wall Street—not one of the top houses, to be sure, but an eminently respectable one. And, unlike the stereotyped stockbroker who hated his job, Joe was lucky enough to be doing just what he wanted to be doing.

The market fascinated him. Money and its manipulation was a source of endless interest to Joe Robshaw. He didn't make a tremendous salary but everything he could afford went into the market. And he was sharp—he almost always made a profit in any speculative venture he went into. It was his business and his hobby all at once.

Now he was lost. General Mining was working for a merger and he was short on three hundred shares. Any information on the prospective merger was of the utmost importance to him. He had to decide whether to stay where he was or whether it would be best to cover.

And he couldn't even understand what the damned article was saying.

He tried again, then gave up and folded the paper neatly, then put it on the floor beside his chair. He looked across the room at Roz and wondered what she was thinking. He could never tell what she was thinking now, not lately. She seemed to be living in a different world.

"Honey—"

She looked up. "What's the matter?"

"I don't know. Can't keep my mind on what I'm reading. Can't concentrate worth a damn."

"Want me to put the TV on?"

He shook his head, waiting for her to come to him and talk to him. But she didn't. She just picked up her book and went on reading. He looked at her for a moment, then shook his head in annoyance and picked up the newspaper. Painfully he groped his way through the article until he managed to figure out that everything was very tentative so far, that it could go either way. His best bet was to sit tight and wait for something to break.

He put the paper aside again. Something was on her mind now and he was damned if he could figure it out. All he knew was that things had been getting imperceptibly different ever since they started with that damned-fool club. They sure needed that club. About as much as they needed food poisoning, that was how much they needed it. About as much as they needed cirrhosis of the liver or urinary retention or galloping diarrhea.

Whose idea was it, anyway? He couldn't remember, and after awhile he had to admit that they'd both felt pretty much the same about the notion. What the hell, every book you read or movie you looked at had some guy doing it to some broad. A man got so he wanted something different now and then, but it didn't seem fair to cheat on your wife.

So *this* seemed fair? Well, it did at first. Hell, he had to admit it sounded pretty damned good at the start. A different woman every two weeks, no strings attached, no hiding anything from the missus. And it was nice stuff at the beginning—a woman coming to him like he was a Greek god or something, showing him one hell of a good time in the hay.

Oh, it bothered him, too—the idea that some son of a bitch was doing the same thing to Roz that he was doing to the broad he was with. But you got used to that sort of thing. Maybe that was the bad part, that you got used to it. Maybe there were some things a man just wasn't supposed to get used to.

He picked up his pipe from the coffee table, looked around for his tobacco pouch, filled the pipe bowl with tobacco and tamped it in snug. The pipe was a Barling made

in England and the tobacco was good plain Kentucky bur-
ley without any of the perfume in it that they loused up so
much good tobacco with. He lit the pipe with a wooden
match, lighting the tobacco evenly all around. It tasted good
and he smoked for several minutes without thinking about
anything but the simple act of drawing the smoke in and
blowing it out.

Yes, it had been good at first. But it wasn't so good any
more. For one thing, he just wasn't taking much interest in
the women lately. Take the last one—Nedra Marshall. A
beautiful girl, youngest one in the group, young and fresh
and good at it. Well, he did what he was supposed to do to
her, but he was damned if he had much fun doing it. The
novelty wore off after awhile. A man just wanted to be back
with his own woman and the hell with the rest of it.

Now his own woman didn't even want it, and wasn't
that one hell of a note? Walking around with her feet a few
inches off the ground, hardly knowing what was going on,
not hearing half the things he said to her. It was no wonder
he couldn't keep his mind on stocks and bonds. It's no mean
trick caring about pieces of paper when your wife doesn't
seem to care about you any more.

Kids might have made a difference. He flushed, knowing that it was his fault they hadn't been able to have children. He couldn't help feeling guilty about it. Hell, there
was something wrong with a man who couldn't get his own
wife knocked up.

Kids would have made a difference. Sure, with a baby around the house they'd be one hell of a lot closer. Would have given them something in common, something to spend their time on together. They never would have gotten mixed up in the damned club in the first place if he'd had the stuff to get a baby growing inside of her.

He drew on his pipe. It had gone out and he lit it again. After a few puffs he noticed that it didn't taste right and knocked it out in a heavy brass ashtray. Maybe it wasn't the fault of the pipe. Maybe he just had a bad taste going in his mouth.

He stood up, his feet a little unsteady, a heavy weight pressing on his shoulders. He walked over to her and she looked up at him.

"Might as well see what's on television," he said.

She didn't object. He walked to the set and they watched a bunch of cowboys kill a bunch of Indians.

JACKSON PIERCE WAS THINKING about the human body. As an athlete he had been blessed with a particularly good body, much as his wife had been blessed with an extraordinary body for her particular brand of athletics.

But he wasn't thinking about bodies in this way. He was thinking instead about the human body in general and what a marvelous machine it was. Every part functioning smoothly for the well-being of the organism as a whole. A machine capable of thinking, acting, running, walking, talking, breathing, building, destroying. A machine that could urinate, defecate, or fornicate. A machine that could do damn near anything but fly, when you came right down to it. And that would probably figure out a way to do that if it worked on it long enough.

But the astounding thing was the adaptability of the human body. Feed it a poison and it would absorb it. Feed it a substandard diet and it would learn to live on rice three times a day.

Feed it alcohol and you would turn into an alcoholic. But you wouldn't kill yourself. Your body chemistry would change a little at a time until you walked around with alcohol in your veins; alcohol instead of blood. But you kept walking around. You didn't die of it—no matter how hard you tried.

"Bad one?"

He looked up.

"You're drinking it straight," Linda was saying. "Usually you spill a little water in it for laughs. So I figured it must be a bad one, whatever it is."

He finished his drink.

"You don't say much. When I married you I didn't know you weren't going to talk to me. That wasn't part of our bargain."

"Lots of things weren't."

"Really? You're being subtle, Jackson. Spell it out for little Linda."

His lip curled. "You're the big intellect. Figure it out for yourself."

"Nasty, aren't you?"

"Promiscuous, aren't you?"

She laughed. It was not a pleasant laugh. It was thin and high-pitched, a nervous laugh, a shrill laugh. It tore him inside and he healed the wound with more liquor. Liquor was a great wound healer. And alcohol was a damned fine antiseptic.

"Promiscuous," she echoed finally. "Promiscuous. A fine word to call a wife."

"You prefer round-heeled? Nymphomaniacal? Sex-mad? Hot to trot? Tell me what you want me to call you. I'll be glad to oblige."

"Try human."

He looked at her. Human, at that point, was about the last thing he could call her. He looked at her too-perfect body, the firm breasts, the thighs, the behind. He looked at her soft white neck and he wanted to wrap his large hands around it and choke the life out of her.

"Human," she said. "Jackson, you knew what you were getting into when you married me. And you knew everybody else was getting into it too. I didn't change. I happen to like sex. I always have and I always will."

"Like it? It's the only thing in the world you like. It's your sole pleasure."

"It's my hobby."

"Hobby? It's your religion."

She laughed at that. It was the same laugh and it made him pour himself another drink and throw it down his throat. This time he didn't even so much as taste it. It proceeded directly from glass to stomach without stopping in his mouth.

"Look," she said, "you have no cause for complaints. You knew what I was like."

"I thought you'd change."

"You should have known better. You know, you never used to sound off like this at me. I acted the same as I do now and you didn't use to raise such a stink about it. I wonder what's bugging you."

Lots of things were bugging him. Nothing, however, that he cared to talk about with her.

"I know," she said, thoughtfully. "You haven't been the same since you went a few rounds with Roz Robshaw last week. *If* you did anything. You haven't been too grand in the hay lately, sweetie. Is that the trouble? Did you crap out and leave Roz all frustrated?"

That was so far from the truth that he would have laughed, except for the one small fact that didn't see anything very funny about it.

"Poor little Jackson," she cooed. "Not much of a man. Not much of a man at all. Can't get it up much lately, can you? Hell, even if I didn't like getting it from all sides I'd have to go out for it the way you've been acting lately. You haven't done me a damned bit of good. You just get stinking drunk and lie there snoring while I'm itching with it."

"You're always itching."

"And you're always snoring. Maybe you're a fag, Jackson. Maybe you'd rather be bouncing around with a nice young boy. Is that it? Are you gay as a jay, Jackson honey?"

"Get off my back."

"Why, I'm just—"

"Leave me alone."

"—trying to help, darling. You're my husband, and a good wife is supposed to stick by her husband through thick and thin. That's what it says in the book. So I'm supposed to stick by you even if you are a lousy mincing sonofabitch of a fag with—"

The rest of her sentence remains unrecorded. At that particular point in the conversation an openhanded roundhouse right caught her on the point of the chin and carried her part way across the room. She did not wake up for quite awhile.

More liquor spilled into the glass and went from the glass to the stomach. It was absorbed from the intestines into the bloodstream, circulated to the brain and dimmed the levels of consciousness. Jackson sat in the chair, drinking, letting his mind wander. His mind wandered thoughtfully and slowly and lonely as a cloud.

If there had been any latent truth in her accusation he might have been angry. There wasn't, and he hadn't been.

He had hit her not in anger but because that was the only way he knew to shut her up once she got going. And it was certainly worthwhile to shut her up. Just sitting and listening to the silence was a pleasure after a conversation with Linda.

The only words that had hurt had been about Roz Robshaw. Roz was a hell of a fine woman and Linda had no business babbling on about her. He felt a lot closer to Roz than he did to Linda, that was for sure. And he liked her a damn sight more.

Now he was thinking about their lovemaking that night a week ago. It had been good, very good, but that was only a small part of it. The big thing was that he realized fully for the first time how miserable a life he and Linda had together. He realized it because one night with Roz had demonstrated what a wonderful thing it could be when a man and a woman proved capable of understanding one another. It made a difference. It wasn't sexual, not sexual at all. It was human.

Now I'm getting philosophical, he thought. That was something Linda could handle a lot better. She was the bright one.

And maybe Linda's philosophy was the right one, the reasonable one, the one that gave a person the best chance for success and peace and happiness. It was a simple philosophy, one of those homespun truths that went over big in Iowa.

It went like this: If you get laid often enough, life can be worth living.

Maybe that was the right way to look at things. Maybe that was a lot better than trying to drink yourself into the grave. You could pour only so much booze down your gullet. You could pour it down and put it away and store some more in your hollow leg, but in the end you were sober once more and the world was still there throwing rocks at you. You could either dodge the rocks or throw rocks back or wave a white flag at the bastards.

Either way you got your head knocked in.

So maybe little Linda had the right idea. Slowly he stood up and walked over to her. She was breathing regularly and he sensed that she would wake up in a minute or two. And he had no overwhelming desire to be in the same room with her when she did.

But first he bent over and removed her blouse. As usual there was no bra beneath it. He rolled her flat on her back and looked down at her breasts. He pinched the nipples and they stiffened. This struck him as mildly hilarious—even when she was totally unconscious she got hot as a stove the minute you laid a hand on her.

He straightened up, a little unsteady on his feet now, the liquor beginning to get to him. It was time for him to lumber upstairs and pass out, but first he wanted to try a quiet and small and probably insignificant experiment. It involved her breasts.

He stared at them. They were magnificent breasts, everything that breasts could be. Pure white, flawless, firm as marble even when she was lying flat on her back with her muscles relaxed. The nipples were a deep red and they contrasted beautifully with the white flesh.

The breasts were perfect. They couldn't be better. They were as large as they could possibly be without being too large.

They were breasts to write home about. Breasts to go into orbit over. Something nice to hang onto in a storm. Firm and soft and smooth.

He stared at them now, stared long and hard at them, noticed how perfect they were.

And he felt nothing.

When he first met her, one look at them was enough to set him off. Touching them sent his pulse racing. The first time he had her on a blanket in the middle of nowhere with the ground under them and the sky over them, the feel of those bare breasts under his hairy chest was so wonderful, so absolutely great that it drove him wild.

He had virtually married her for her breasts. Now he felt nothing. Nothing at all.

Less than nothing.

Sick, drunk, exhausted, he carried himself up the long staircase and collapsed fully dressed on the bed.

He slept soundly, if not well.

Chapter 4

Larry Carson couldn't sleep.

He wanted to sleep. He was tired, damned tired after one perfect hell of a day at the office, a day that managed to take up a good part of the night as well. An idiot conference, predicated on the well known premise that two empty heads are better than one, had kept him in Manhattan for a tasteless dinner and a long, long barrel of blah after dinner.

He came home from Manhattan wishing softly that he would never have to go back there again. He'd been making good money. If only he could save a dime now and then he could tell Neil and McCowan where to shove themselves and get as far from the New York metropolitan area as was humanly possible. The bustling little banality of Eastport certainly wasn't far enough.

Some nice out of the way place where people let you alone. Maine, maybe, or northern Vermont. A place where he could go fishing now and then, a place where he could wander alone in pine forests and smell real grass. Not a mess of creeping bent trying to creep around crab grass, for Christ's sad sake.

So home he came, aching for the peace he found with

his wife, and then what had happened? Virtually nothing had happened. Sue had been home all right. She was sitting in the pine-paneled study in a brown study all her own, turning the pages of a book without seeming to read the words. Not exactly the hearty welcome that the American male was supposed to get when he came home from the office. Just a wave of the hand for a hello.

He'd wanted to talk to her. She was the perfect wife, a woman who took complete interest in his work, who knew the men in his office solely from his descriptions but who knew them very well because she listened to him so attentively.

But not lately.

Every day she was retreating into some far-off corner of the globe uninhabited save for her own murky soul. Every day she was talking less to him, looking less frequently at him, spending less time with him. It wasn't as if she was doing something herself. She was simply doing nothing at all, delving into her own psyche, losing all touch with his half of the world.

So he sat by himself, worked his way through the inevitably monotonous hoopla of *Advertising Age*, wondering why all the other ad men in the world were such dolts, wishing he was away in Maine or Vermont with nothing to do but fish and wander.

Eventually they went to bed. He got in under the covers and waited for her but she seemed to be taking an unusually long time in the bathroom. It was almost as though she wanted to avoid him, wanted him to fall asleep before she came to join him.

An unpleasant thought.

But, of course, he did not drop off to sleep. And when she came to him it was not good at all, which was ridiculous because it was always good with him and Sue, always fresh and exciting and stimulating and rewarding, always something very personal and special and private and sweet.

This time it was bad.

He took her in his arms and she buried her face in his shoulder. He was tender with her, more tender than usual because of her particular mood, and he was basically a very tender person to begin with. It didn't seem consistent with the flippancy he presented to the world, with the brash hard-guy approach which had pushed him to the top in such a short time.

It was the way he was. The tenderness, fundamental in his particular personality, was something he saved for his wife. This is why, in a sense, the club activities never really touched him. It was the Outer Self, the Image, that made love to other men's wives. The Inner Man, the tender and thoughtful person who was the genuine Larry Carson, was a different sort of article. He hid most of the time. He emerged only when he was alone, alone with the woman he loved.

So he kissed her, very tenderly, and rolled her over onto

her back so that he could hold her breasts in his hands. He touched them and kissed them, repeating the pattern of lovemaking which seemed the perfect sort of lovemaking to him, familiar without ever being routine, patterned without being regimented, tender and gentle and sweet from beginning to end.

Except that, this time, there was something missing.

Her responses were wrong, for one thing. There seemed to be something missing for her, and when it was over and he lay very still in the warm sweet shelter of her body, he knew that he had failed, that he had not brought her to complete fulfillment, that a part of her was still locked in its own private world.

Then he heard her words. He heard them right the first time and they half-tore him apart, but he asked her to repeat them on the chance that his ears were playing nasty games with him.

"I didn't feel a thing."

And, because he was a husband who loved his wife, he wanted to talk about it. He wanted to find out what was the matter, what was wrong with her, what might be wrong with him. He wanted to get right down to the roots of the trouble and fix everything up.

But she did not want to talk. She wanted to sleep, she said, and seconds later she rolled over and dropped off to sleep without another word. At least she seemed to sleep. It was no use talking to her, no use trying to iron out whatever the problems might be.

He, of course, did not sleep.

A more secure man might have slept. A more secure man might have written the episode off as the product of mental and/or emotional exhaustion, a temporary thing, an unimportant thing that would heal of its own accord. A more secure man might have slept, and so might a less introspective, analytical man. That sort of man might have brushed the statement aside because of the inability to face unpleasant thoughts.

Larry Carson was not a secure man. He was not an emotionally evasive man. He was a man who thought a lot and who worried a lot.

So he did not sleep. Instead he thought.

And worried.

The thinking part of the process was largely a matter of remembering recent events with a new perspective. In the light of what she had just said, little things that he had noticed only partially became much more significant than they had seemed at the time. He had to admit that there had been something out of kilter in their lovemaking for quite a little while now, something distant in her attitude, something wrong with their relationship.

He hadn't noticed it, not consciously. But now he saw it in perspective and wondered how in God's name he could have missed it the first time around.

It seemed obvious now.

He traced it back as closely as he could, figuring that it

had started roughly ten days ago when he had gone home from the party with Nancy Gordon while Sue had wound up with that Phillips weasel.

Mark Phillips.

Larry had never liked Mark Phillips. There was one hell of a lot hidden within Phillips and Larry had been able to see that something was always concealed. He couldn't see what it was—he hadn't looked that closely—but it was something. It was almost as though Mark Phillips were two people at once, two very different people living together in one body under one name.

Half of Phillips was like a sweet little old lady. The other half, he felt certain, was something very different. Something sinister.

And, he knew intuitively, when the sweet little lady went out like a light, something dreadful would appear. Sort of a Jekyll-and-Hyde syndrome.

But what did that have to do with Sue?

That was the question and he was damned if he knew the answer. He wished suddenly that his brother Dave were around so that he could sit down and talk the whole mess out with him. Dave would understand. Dave was a writer and in his writing he quite often came up with characters along the lines of Phillips, twisted little men with something all shot to hell inside of them.

But Dave was off in Mexico getting a quickie divorce and an even quicker remarriage. He had to get through this by himself, work it out alone until it added up to something that made a little more in the way of sense to him. Now it made no sense at all. Something was wrong but it was hard to tell what.

He blamed himself, Sue, and Phillips. Himself because he was certain that, in some way or other, he was failing Sue as a lover. He was doing something wrong, though God alone knew what it might be. He wasn't being the husband to her that he wanted to be, that he always thought he had been in the past.

But how, he wondered, do you tally up a man's performance between the sheets? How do you keep score in the game of love? There were all the old yardsticks of natural equipment, staying power and ingenuity, but he had a strong hunch that these weren't making the difference in this particular case. It was something else, something he was suddenly doing wrong.

He blamed Phillips, not for what he might or might not have been, but because he had been the catalyst in the chemical change of their marriage. Phillips, whether or not through any fault of his own, had loused things up. Larry blamed him, and hated him silently but thoroughly, hated him with a hatred rooted in his own feelings of inadequacy.

Finally, he blamed his wife. It couldn't all be his fault. Part of it was hers. She could tell him, communicate with him, let him know what the hell was going on. Theirs had always been an inordinately close marriage, a sharing of experience, and it wasn't like her to crawl off into a shell and hide herself from him. Not like her at all. The hiding, more than the bedroom failure, was what really had him worried.

He lay in darkness, smoking too many cigarettes, listening to the slow and even breathing from her side of the bed. He had a longing to reach over and shake her, to get something straight between them once and for all. But, perhaps because his own feelings of failure were so deep, he stayed where he was and left her to herself.

And, slowly, his feelings changed.

To anger.

He was hurt, deeply hurt. And the hurt had to heal, and the healing process demanded a psychological inner revenge. He took this revenge by feeling angry with her, by telling himself that he was certainly okay in the hay, that Nancy Gordon hadn't complained noticeably, that nobody complained, that something was wrong with Sue and maybe she should take herself and go to hell, go straight to hell, do not pass go, do not collect two hundred dollars.

Saturday.

Saturday was meeting night, party night, hot pillow night. And suddenly he was looking forward to Saturday, looking forward much more desperately than usual to the chance of bedding down with another woman.

It was a duel now, a duel between himself and the world that was closing down around him. He would be a willing participant in the duel.

He even knew what his weapon would be. Not a gun exactly. Not a sword, not quite.

Sort of a combination of the two.

He held his weapon in his hand like a pimpled boy and, finally, drifted off to an unpleasant sort of sleep.

Chapter 5

EVERYBODY LOVES SATURDAY NIGHT.

It was a very nice Saturday night. It should have been, because it had been an incredibly fine Saturday. Saturdays in Eastport are lazy days. The men are home from the office and the children are home from school. The men sleep late, wake up with hangovers, chase the hangovers with Benzedrine and lie around the house thinking of all the things they ought to do but haven't the slightest intention of doing. Rugs are not beaten, asphalt tile is not laid, lawns are not mowed, gardens are not planted.

The sky was cloudy enough to keep the sun from making itself obnoxious. The clouds were white puffs of fluff—or at least, they looked that way from the ground. If you had ever been in an airplane that flew through a cloud you felt differently about them. You knew then that they were, after all, just pea-soup fog floating in the middle of the air. You could never look at them in quite the same way again.

But whatever they were, they kept the sun out without darkening the sky. Which, all things considered, was all anyone expected them to do.

By the time the sun got tired of hanging around, the

day could have passed for summer. The air had an almost tropical taste and touch to it, heavy and sensual, sultry. The night that followed the day was even lazier than the day it followed. The trees with their new and bright green leaves on them were motionless in the incredibly calm air. Smoke rose from a cigarette in an unknown column that ascended skyward as straight as a die. The moon was an orange ball shining through a murky haze. There were no stars visible.

At 8:39 the Gordons arrived at Walter and Mary Forsythe's home. They were the first. The last arrivals, Bill and Pidge Jansen, entered the Forsythe house at 9:22. By 10:05 everybody was working on his or her second drink.

Bit by bit the evening began to get in the mood. Joe Robshaw, very depressed and a little rocky with a pair of drinks under his belt, got Pidge Jansen off in a corner and began to explain just how boring everything was. Pidge decided that she knew a sure cure for boredom. She took one of Joe's hands and tucked it neatly up under her full skirt. Because Pidge had developed an aversion to underwear, Joe's hand was the only thing beneath the skirt.

Well, almost the only thing.

Jackson Pierce, more sober than usual for a change, was trying to talk to Roz Robshaw. That was all he wanted to do. He just wanted to talk to her, for Christ's sake. Conversation proved somewhat difficult, however, because Steve Gordon had stationed himself behind Roz and had one hand on each of her breasts. The things he was doing with his infernally clever hands were playing hell with the conversation.

While Jackson Pierce was trying to talk, words were the furthest thing from the mind of his lovely wife Linda. She had managed to latch onto Don Marshall, who in turn had demonstrated remarkable willingness to be latched onto. The two of them had been blessed with the good fortune of being able to capture a couch which they were busy breaking in.

The couch was a long one, designed so that four people could sit comfortably on it. Now, however, nobody was sitting on it. Instead, two people were lying on it.

Don and Linda.

An impartial observer would have thought that there was something wrong with them. They looked for all the world as though they were making love, except for one slight difficulty. All of their clothing was still on. The impartial observer might have conjectured that they were too drunk to bother with clothing, and as a result were having considerable trouble in accomplishing their obvious objective. The truth of the matter was that they were going through what is known colloquially as a dry run. Just sort of getting into practice you might say.

Larry Carson, bearded and belligerent, had abandoned his wife the minute they entered the house. When Nedra Marshall wandered into his line of vision he grabbed her as if he was afraid she might run away. Ned had no intentions of running away, as it turned out. When he plumped himself into a chair, she plumped herself right down on his lap and looked down at him.

Ned was wearing a delightfully low-cut blouse, and when she looked down at Larry and shrugged slightly, two very nice breasts left the blouse and came out into the open. During what followed Ned kept up a running stream of chatter, talking about anything and everything that entered her alleged mind. Larry, on his part, listened to everything she said and never attempted a word. He was, above all else, a gentleman.

And a gentleman never talks with his mouth full.

Mary Forsythe and Bill Jansen had managed to get together, after a fashion. The notion of sleeping with an older woman was terrifying and exciting at once to Bill. Mary, on her part, was amused while sharing his excitement. And, because she knew what surprise Walt had in store for all of them, the practiced caresses Bill used on her were even more stimulating than they would ordinarily have been.

Peggy Phillips sat by herself. She was watching Mary and Bill.

Her heart was pounding.

Mark Phillips sat in the middle of a loveseat with a woman on either side of him. He was having a very good time. He had his left arm around Nancy Gordon, his right arm around Sue Carson. He had his left hand on Nancy Gordon's left breast and his right hand on Sue Gordon's right breast. He was squeezing both breasts, but there was a difference in the two actions. His left hand manipulated Nancy's breast gently, skillfully. His right hand tightened on Sue's breast until she had to use all her will power to keep from crying out.

Mark was enjoying himself. And both Nancy and Sue were having the time of their lives.

When Walt returned to the room and began clapping for order they tactfully ignored him one and all. Eventually they gave up what they were doing and let him talk. And he talked, albeit mysteriously.

"Come with me," he announced. "All of you."

And, finally, they followed him. He led them upstairs to a very large room in the rear of the house. The room was empty. Instead of chairs, pillows had been placed on the rug in various spots. He told them to sit down on the pillows. They sat down and looked around, amused.

Music started playing. It was impossible to pinpoint the location of the speaker. The music seemed to be coming out of all four walls at once until it enveloped them in a melodic haze. It was strange music. The rhythms were persistent, the harmonies atonal.

Walt walked to the front of the room. He pulled down a white screen.

"Home movies," he said. "Every suburban party should be graced with home movies."

Some of the men and women seated on the floor were

completely lost. Others, a little cleverer, had a pretty good idea what was coming next.

Walt walked away from the screen. The music swelled up and the audience waited for something to happen. The air was thick, haunted by the smell of some unfamiliar and musky perfume.

Slowly, very slowly, the lights dimmed and went out entirely. A movie projector whirred from somewhere in the back of the room.

The show began.

Title Card: ANXIOUS TO PLEASE

Camera pans a bedroom, moves in for a medium shot of a woman sitting on the edge of the bed. She is a big woman with long dark hair. She is wearing a sweater and skirt. Her feet are bare.

The camera moves in, focuses on the front of the sweater. There is evidently nothing under the sweater other than the woman. The sweater is very tight the woman's breasts are extremely large.

Full shot of the woman.

Title Card: "I WISH HE'D HURRY UP."

Door opens. The woman looks, up, an expectant smile on her face. When she sees who it is the smile dies. Her visitor is a trim young Negro girl wearing an apron. She is, evidently, the maid.

Title Card: "I FINISHED THE WALLS, MA'AM. DO YOU WANT ME TO WAX THE FLOOR?"

The camera moves in for a shot of the Negro girl. Besides the apron she is wearing a light cotton dress and a pair of tennis shoes. The dress is short and her legs are very attractive.

Title Card: "COME HERE, VIRGINIA."

The girl walks to the woman. The woman seems displeased with the way the girl is wearing the apron. She rearranges it, and so doing her hands brush the girl's body, hesitating slightly when they touch the breasts and hips. There is a slow dreamy smile on the Negro girl's face.

Title Card: "YES, DO THE FLOOR. AND IF A MAN COMES SEND HIM RIGHT UP."

The girl nods and leaves the room. She wiggles when she walks and the camera follows her. Then the camera dollies in for an extreme close up of the woman's face. She seems to be thinking about something.

Title Card: "SHE'S PRETTY BUT I'M PRETTIER."

As if to prove it, the woman stands up and begins to disrobe. First she pulls the sweater free from her skirt and takes its off. She cups her breasts in her hands and inspects them carefully. Then she smiles, evidently pleased with them.

Her skirt comes next. The slip beneath it is black and thin and lacy. When the woman stands up and walks around the room, the camera dollies for a shot of her with a bright lamp behind her. From such an angle the slip hides none of her attractive features.

The woman removes the slip and the camera moves up for an extra shot of her abdomen. The woman begins stroking herself with one hand. Her fingernails are very long.

Title Card: "GOD, I WISH HE'D HURRY!!!"

The camera pans for a medium shot of the door. It opens slowly and a man walks in. He is very tall with broad shoulders and a stubble of beard on his chin. He wears a white tee-shirt and a pair of soiled dungarees. There is an anchor tattooed on one forearm.

His expression as he gazes at the woman is one of obvious hunger. He approaches her quickly, shedding his clothes en route.

Title Card: "HERE IT COMES, HONEY!"

The man and woman are naked. She stretches out on the bed, lying flat on her back, her eyes shut, her breasts rising and falling with her rapid and intense breathing.

The man joins her on the bed.

Chapter 6

ROZ ROBSHAW FELT SICK to her stomach. Really, genuinely, physically ill. She wanted to vomit her guts out, to keep on heaving until there was nothing left to throw up in her stomach.

And yet she went on watching the movie.

It was disgusting. It was worse than disgusting. It was depraved and sick and warped and twisted.

But she couldn't help watching it.

It wasn't as though she wanted to watch it. She didn't. She wanted to go somewhere else and be noisily ill. But the fascination of the movie was too much for her. She could only sit on the soft pillow and watch the evil images on the screen while the weird and wild music wrapped itself around her and caressed her.

She couldn't understand herself. She wasn't a teenager, easily excited by anything smacking of forbidden sin. She was a mature woman, a married woman, a woman who had had enough of sex to distinguish between the genuine article and the nonsense parading around on the screen. Yet there was no denying the hold it had on her, the excitement it brought her, the way it made her shake and tremble inside like a Japanese paper hut in an earthquake. She might have been amused by it, or interested, or bored—any of these reactions made sense.

But excited?

That didn't make sense. The strange combination of unnatural excitement and unnatural nausea was driving her out of her mind. In one sense she couldn't watch another minute of it; in quite another sense she could not tear her eyes from the screen for a single moment.

And Steve was not helping.

She'd submitted willingly enough to Steve's caresses in the living room. It was all part of the game then, and his hands on her breasts had been pleasant enough. But now they were working together with the movie, and the result was far too moving, far too exciting to be pleasant. It was frightening.

Steve was being damned clever about it. Whatever went on the screen, Steve would attempt to duplicate in the flesh. When the woman cupped her own breasts, Steve held her breasts in his hands. When the woman shifted her attention to another part of her body, Steve's attention shifted correspondingly.

And she liked it. Christ, how she liked it! She didn't even object when Steve's agile fingers found the waistband of her silk panties and drew them down and off. It just made everything that much more exciting.

When the woman on the screen was joined by the man,

the whole thing was too damned much for Roz to bear. She couldn't take it. The further they carried things, the further she herself was carried.

Her passion rose higher.

And higher.

And higher still . . . until release of some sort had become a simple biological necessity.

She clenched her teeth until they ached. Then, her eyes still riveted to the images on the screen, she grabbed Steve's head between her strong hands and forced him into a position that would bring her the fulfillment she needed.

"Hey!"

She didn't answer him.

"I can't see the movie like this," he complained. "I can't see a thing."

She thought to herself that he could see plenty, plenty for him to do what he had to do. And she locked his head in place and told him that if he didn't do what she wanted him to do she would gouge his eyes out with her thumbs.

In which case, she added gently, he would almost definitely miss the rest of the movie.

Title Card: "ONE MORE TIME!"

The man and woman make love, "one more time" in a new manner. This is their third time. The picture required four successive days to film, but of course the audience is in no position to know this. It seems as though the man and woman are engaging in a completely non-stop sort of orgy. No sooner have they finished making love than they begin again.

The third time, like the others, is filled with interesting camera angles and close-ups. The man and woman are photographed from every conceivable position. The result is a vaguely three-dimensional effect; to the audience, it seems almost as though the movie is a live exhibition and the man and woman are performing in the room with them.

They finish. The man rolls free of the woman and lies on his back, evidently exhausted. The woman, too, seems to have had sufficient sexual exercise for the moment. She is lying on her side, her face to the camera, her mouth gaping open and her eyes shut.

Long shot of the door, opening. The Negro girl enters, still wearing her apron.

Title Card: "I FINISHED THE FLOOR, MA'AM."

The girl's face as she sees the man and the woman on the bed. She turns and heads for the door, but the man is too fast for her. He leaps off the bed and races to her, catching her before she can get out the door. Then, his hand gripping her forearm painfully, he drags her over toward the bed.

Shot of man's face.

Title Card: "WHO IS SHE?"

Shot of woman's face.

Title Card: "SHE'S JUST THE MAID."

Shot of man's face.

Title Card: "I WANT HER. GIVE ME A HAND WITH HER."

Shot of girl's face, terror stricken.

Title Card: "NO! NO! NO!"

The girl struggles valiantly, but the man and woman work together as a team and prove too much for her. The two of them manage to get her clothes off and pin her down on the bed.

The camera pans her body. Her breasts are small but well-formed, her stomach flat, her thighs well made.

The man makes love to her while she struggles and appears to scream. Behind him the woman watches, her face wreathed in weird smiles.

Periodically the man stops and strikes the girl with his hand. Each time he does this the camera focuses on her face. Her expression is one of great suffering, and her pain evidently add immeasurably to the man's enjoyment.

Once again, as usual, the camera examines the situation from every conceivable angle, giving the audience a full picture of the tableaux on the screen.

Chapter 7

WALT FORSYTHE, WHO DID not have a woman to himself when the picture began, managed to acquire Nancy Gordon in the interim. As you may remember, she started out with Mark Phillips, more or less sharing him with Sue Carson. But bit by bit Mark shifted his attention entirely to Larry Carson's wife, giving her the sort of caresses which he liked to apply and which she liked to receive. It was a simple matter for Walt to get Nancy to himself.

The first thing he did was to remove all of Nancy's clothing.

The second thing he did was to remove all of his own clothing.

And then, with the air of a master instructing an inquisitive pupil, he began to fill Nancy in on some of the fine points of sex.

She was certainly ready. Mark's caresses had excited her a bit, and the movie had excited her a bit more, and the music certainly hadn't hurt any. Under any other set of circumstances she might have objected to the things Walt wanted to do to her and to the things he wanted her to do to him.

Now she did not object in the least. On the contrary,

her own enthusiasm for the unusual seemed at least equal to his. The more depraved and perverted any particular act was, the more she craved it, the more she enjoyed it, the deeper her passion as she participated in it. Walt had the exhilarating experience of transforming a relatively normal girl into a hungry insatiable slut.

He liked the change in her. He liked the things she did to him and the things he in turn did to her. He liked the terrifying little moans that started deep in her throat and exploded in his ears. He liked it when her teeth sank into him, and he liked it when his teeth in turn bit her flesh until her moans turned to screams.

He quickly forgot the picture. He forgot the music as well. He preferred real human sex to movies, and what he was getting from Nancy Gordon was about as real and human as anything could be.

He felt his heart beginning to pound and the blood beat against his brain like a thousand drummers beating a million drums as hard as they could. It was good, very good, very very very good, too good to stop.

And for a moment he thought he was going to die.

He was afraid. His heart was not good, according to several doctors, and one of these days it would simply run out of gas. He was supposed to live the quiet life, avoid too much exercise, take things easy.

If the doctor could see him now—

But it was worth it. God, it was worth it. If he had to

give this up he might as well be dead. If he couldn't match a woman's passion with passion of his own there was little point in living.

And what a way to go—

It got better, and better, and even better. The only sound in the world was the beating of own heart. It was louder than her moans, louder than the other sounds from other couples that filled the room and drowned out the sensual music.

Louder.

Faster.

Harder . . .

And then, suddenly, after a sensation that was agonizingly wonderful, everything stopped. Just stopped. And he thought that he was dead.

He came back to consciousness a moment or two later, his head cushioned on a warm breast, her hands caressing and massaging his shoulders. And he knew that he was alive, that he had managed to live through another one, a very good one.

He sighed, relieved.

And he wondered how many more women he would be able to have before he quite literally screwed himself to death.

On the screen the man finally finishes with the Negro girl. He leaves her lying prone on the bed, gets up grinning from ear to ear, and begins to put on his clothes. When he is dressed he walks over to the woman and gives her an affectionate pinch. The camera follows him as far as the door. Then he closes the door and the camera moves in for a shot of the woman.

Title Card: "THE POOR THING."

The woman crouches over the girl, examining her to see if she has been badly hurt. The woman runs her hand over the girl's silken flesh, starting with her stomach, then moving upward to her breasts. She touches the breasts softly, fondling them, pinching the nipples very gently. Her hands keep moving.

Title Card: "MINE ARE BIGGER BUT HERS ARE NICE!"

The girl seems to be unconscious. The woman crouches over her now, bending so that her own breasts touch the breasts of the girl. Slowly she moves her body first to one side and then to the other so that her big breasts brush back and forth over the breasts of the girl.

Title Card: "POOR VIRGINIA."

Now the woman begins to use her mouth on the girl's breasts. She is very efficient in this respect and the caresses seem to have the effect of restoring the girl to the world of the living. The girl opens her eyes. She likes what the woman is doing. The woman continues for awhile, then the camera switches to a shot of the girl's face, talking.

Title Card: "MY TURN."

The girl gives similar caresses to the woman, using her lips on the woman's large breasts. The woman is not content to play a passive role and finds things to do to the girl at the same time.

The camera has a field day now, switching all over the place for a good many unlikely and interesting pictures.

Shot of the woman's face.

Title Card: "NOW BOTH OF US."

The woman and the girl arrange themselves on the bed in the traditional position of lesbian love.

They begin.

If Peggy Phillips had happened to have a knife, it is altogether probable that she would have slashed her wrists and bled to death in the middle of the nice picture.

If she had had a gun, it is quite possible that she would have blown her brains out.

If she had had a bottle of sleeping pills in her purse, it is more than likely that she would have gobbled up the lot of them.

But she didn't. So, instead, she divided her attention between two things:

The movie and Mary Forsythe.

By the time, the woman and the Negro girl got together it was a little too much. Mary was stark naked with Bill Jansen making love to her valiantly, and Peggy felt her heart jumping up and hitting her square in the teeth. She wanted to scream, to stand up and shriek, to wail like a banshee.

Her mind filled with memories of Andy and bit by bit all the little walls she had constructed began to tumble like a sweet little row of dominoes. Things like home and family and the good American middle class way of life had less and less meaning every minute.

She looked at the movie and at Mary. She thought of Andy and the way Andy alone had been able to make her feel. Mark never made her feel that good. Mark never would.

He couldn't.

He was a man.

And suddenly she knew for a fact what she had never been willing to admit. Knew it inside and out, backwards and forward, up and down. Knew it so completely that it frightened her and disgusted her and made her wish desperately for her own death.

She was a lesbian.

Not bisexual, not AC-DC. An out-and-out lesbian, a woman who would only be happy with another woman for a lover. A woman who had no right to live a normal life because she herself was anything but normal.

A lesbian.

There were many names for what she was. Lesbian, dyke, queer, butch, lady lover.

Unpleasant names, names that were not nice at all. Names that made her want to kill herself quickly so that all the aches inside her would cease aching once and for all.

Names that fit.

She turned from the screen and devoted all her attention to Mary. Bill Jansen was doing things to her, strange things, and Peggy wanted to take him and scratch his eyes out. He had no right to do those sort of things to her, to Mary. He had no right on earth to do anything to her, to touch her, to kiss her, to be in the same room with her.

He was a man.

A man. A lousy, no-good, rotten sonofabitch of a man.

Damn him! Damn him for playing around with Mary! Damn him to hell!

Mary was naked, and Bill was naked, and Bill was making love to the beautiful woman in such a way that her breasts were exposed and free. It seemed an awful waste for those breasts not to be in use. A horrible waste. Somebody should be holding them, touching them, kissing them.

Peggy caught her breath. She couldn't hold herself back, and yet she knew that Mary would hate her, that Mary would tell the world that Peggy Phillips was a dirty little queer.

She was being torn in two.

Slowly, hardly knowing what she was doing, Peggy removed her own clothing. She stripped all the way down until she was naked as a jay bird. Naked as a jay bird and gay as a jay, she thought hysterically. One sweet hell of a combination.

Then she crawled over to Mary Forsythe. She curled herself in a little ball with her face just inches from Mary's breast. Her lips were actually burning with the desire to kiss those breasts.

Her mouth moved closer.

Closer—

It was insane. Mary would know what was happening, couldn't help knowing what was happening, couldn't avoid realizing that the lips kissing breasts and the lips kissing her elsewhere belonged to two different people. Mary would know and it would all be over before it started and it would be the end of Peggy Phillips' private little world.

But she simply could not help herself.

The first kiss was a chaste peck on the underside of the breast. And Peggy thought that nothing in the world could be so soft, so smooth.

The second kiss was bolder. She took the nipple between her lips and kissed hard.

She could not believe what happened next.

Because Mary's hand reached out, groping for her. And Mary began caressing Peggy's body, touching her, exciting her, helping her along to the crest of passion. Mary liked what she was doing, Mary liked her, Mary liked it, and oh God in heaven how marvelously good it felt, how wonderful it felt, how divine it felt, how sweet, how good, how luscious, how delicious, how grand!

Her heart swelled over. Her eyes filled with tears of relief and joy, and the tears spilled over onto Mary's big soft breast.

She licked them off.

It got better. It was better than anything, better than anything in the world, too good to believe it was so damned good. Better than she had hoped, better than ever, better than any of the times with Andy.

And it did not stop getting better. Not until it happened for her and the world sang and pranced and loudly exploded in a white puff of pleasure.

Contrary to established Hollywood techniques, the movie does not fade out in a blaze of glory. There is no punch ending, no kicker, no twist of the knife. The two participants simply run the length of their own private repertoire and collapse, exhausted.

No tricks, no gimmicks, no man on horse riding off into picture postcard sunset.

Nothing fancy.

Just a basic ending, accomplished by the simple expedient of a title card.

Title Card: THE END.

In a sense the title card is right and in a sense the title card is wrong. A person might argue that this is, in fact, the end.

He might argue, on the other hand, that it is merely the beginning.

Chapter 8

THE PRESSURES OF THE twentieth century have made an ideal of normalness. The idea prevails that if a person is not just like every other person, something is quite obviously the matter with him. Even the word abnormal has inevitable bad connotations, instead of meaning, simply, a divergence from the norm. The man who walks differently or talks differently or dresses differently or, God forbid, thinks differently, is automatically cause for suspicion, investigation, and alienation from the group.

As a result, everybody who has any choice in the matter appears to be absolutely normal, one hundred percent average, a combination of the *Reader's Digest* and *Time Magazine's* view of what the red-blooded American man or woman should think, feel, do and be. Everybody acts "normal," thinks "normal," and feels "normal."

As a result, most people are sick. They stifle their differences in an attempt to make them disappear, and the end-product of all this repression is that these differences are forced beneath the surface where they become warped and twisted. They are still present, still as dynamic as if they lay upon the surface of each individual.

And they come out.

Not always. Sometimes the repression is successful—sometimes the repressed characteristics are buried deep within a person and are never forced to the surface. This is not healthy either and the person leads a less happy life without ever knowing the reason for his unhappiness. But this "successful" repression is certainly less obvious in its sickness than the unsuccessful repression, where stresses and strains, knock the individual apart at the seams.

In which case, of course, the obvious thing happens.

All hell breaks loose.

IT WAS SATURDAY NIGHT and all hell was breaking loose. The combination of movie and orgy, had managed the difficult and subtle task of getting under everybody's skin. Whatever troubled the sixteen persons gathered at Walt and Mary Forsythe's home, there had been some psychic quality in either movie or audience or both to knock the props out from under each and every watcher.

The results were, to say the least, unique.

Peggy Phillips, unable to take the double frontal assault of lesbian action on the screen and sexual activity on the part of her object of desire just a few feet away from her, had suddenly and alarmingly ceased to repress her own homosexuality. Mary Forsythe, always ready for anything, had been receptive. Bill Jansen, who had been making love to Mary before the two women had managed to get together, had been entranced by the spectacle. And he too managed to go off his nut a bit.

Bill Jansen was fundamentally a tremendously sensual person. In adolescence he had masturbated somewhat more than was normal. During college he was a Lothario type, knocking over any woman he could. When no woman was available, fantasies produced by books or movies served as an almost acceptable substitute.

Now everything was coming at him too fast. First he had been watching a movie, a much more graphic movie than anything he had ever before seen. And he watched it not in a room filled with cigar smoke and sweating men but in a room filled with subtle perfumes and subtle music and unsubtle women.

On top of that, there was a woman next to him who was hell on wheels. The combination of the movie and Mary was enough in and of itself. It had him crawling the walls, and then crawling all over Mary. Simply making love to Mary hadn't turned out to be enough. So much stimulation had made him quite insatiable, and he and Mary just stayed right where they were in the middle of the floor and made love over and over and over.

And then, from out of nowhere, Peggy Phillips had materialized. And what she and Mary were doing was precisely what the Negro girl and the woman had been doing on the screen. It was too much for Bill—he couldn't keep straight on the entire situation. He didn't know whether Peggy and

Mary were part of a movie or whether they were really alive. He watched them and touched them and decided that they were alive if he was, but that just gave rise to another problem. Maybe all three of them were characters in some weird movie that a whole bunch of other people were watching. Maybe that was it. You could never tell.

If so, he was left high and dry. That wasn't good. He should be doing something so that the audience could get its money's worth.

He found something to do.

Mary and Peggy were all tangled up. So he stroked both of them, touched their breasts, fondled their thighs, kissed their soft flesh. It gave him something to do and they both seemed to enjoy it. He enjoyed it himself, enjoyed the whole thing tremendously, and every once in a while when things got to be too much for him he found a way to get it out of his system.

And all the while, he hoped that the movie was going well and that the audience was enjoying it. He'd always wanted to be an actor. This was his big chance.

LARRY CARSON HAD BEEN the only one outside of the Forsythes who hadn't been particularly surprised when the movie was shown. Not too many things surprised Larry, and one of the things that couldn't surprise him was anything in the world that Walt Forsythe might do. Larry had figured out long ago that Forsythe was capable of almost any act in the world and a sex movie didn't surprise him at all.

Nor did it excite him especially. He'd seen too many of them in his youth to get excited over one now. Moreover, any vicarious form of sexual titillation is successful only insofar as the person watching is able to forget the artificiality of it and accept it as a suitable substitute for reality. Larry couldn't. To him, the movie remained light cast on a screen through a strip of celluloid, a collection of camera angles and forced responses that didn't move him in the least.

But, while the movie did not move him, the same could hardly be said for Ned Marshall.

Nedra was the young and eager type, and the movie had managed to make her more eager if not any younger. While Larry didn't get much of a kick watching the movie, he got one goddamned living squalling hell of a kick being with Ned while she watched it.

The combination of the two of them was quite a combination. Larry was still hurt from his wife's rejection, filled with feelings of sexual inadequacy, anxious to prove himself both to himself and to the world. Nedra was an incredibly passionate young woman to begin with, and the time she had spent with Larry earlier in the evening had done nothing to dull her spirit. Sex had been a recent discovery for her and she was busy making up for lost time with a vengeance.

When she and Larry finished, it somehow was not enough. She wanted more. So she stood up, stark naked, and let the world know what she wanted.

"Hey," she called, "I want a man!"

Nobody answered her.

"I want a man, dammit. Isn't there a goddamned man anywhere in the goddamned place? What does a girl have to do to get a little attention?"

The question by now was purely rhetorical. Nedra Marshall, young and naked and smelling of sex, was standing with her arms akimbo and her body thrown back, her legs slightly spread and her feet planted on either side of a pillow. Her breasts were on the small side, but they more than made up in shape what they lacked in size. The nipples were tiny coral dots set on mounds of ivory. Her thighs were ivory, too—twin columns of purest white skin, well-muscled, perfectly shaped.

And the way she was standing, her torso thrown back, her long hair hanging down aimed at the floor, her eyes rolling and her mouth a crimson smear, she had no trouble at all in attracting the desired attention. As a matter of fact, more than a few men were already paying attention to her—men who had already made love to her on other Saturday nights and men who had only thought about it and waited for their chance in silence.

This seemed to be their chance.

"Come on, damnit. One at a time, as many of you as want it. Come on, if you're man enough."

Joe Robshaw was taking tentative steps toward the girl. Jackson Pierce was getting slowly to his feet, his eyes on her body.

"This is a switch club, isn't it?" Ned's voice was harsher now, more desperate. There was a weird light in her eyes that had never been there before, or that had never been noticed in the past. "If this is a switch club, what do you say we do a little switching? Come on damn you. Joe, come over here and help a girl out. You look like you ought to be able to give a girl a good time. Come on!"

Joe Robshaw walked to her, his mouth open, his eyes almost vacant. When he neared her she flung herself at him and they tumbled to the floor. It began at once, and at once she began to make noises that rent the room apart. By the time it was over for them she was screaming at the top of her lungs.

Joe rolled away from her, drained. But Nedra had hardly begun.

Jackson Pierce was next . . .

FOR LARRY CARSON, NED'S display was the straw that broke the proverbial back of the proverbial camel. He'd gone to her to prove himself, to ease the hurt to his pride that had resulted from his failure with his wife. And it had been good with Nedra, and when it was over he felt happy, happy that he had been accepted by this vibrant young woman, that he had taken his pleasure with her and that he had brought her fulfillment.

But now—

Now she was taking on all comers, shouting that

she needed a man. He had been a man, or at least he had thought so.

Thought.

Well, he thought wrong. That much was relatively obvious. If you satisfy a woman, he told himself, she does not get up from the floor and holler for somebody else. If you satisfy a woman she just sort of lies there and tells you how good it was, which can be damnably ego-building.

But when all she wants is somebody else to finish the job that you evidently bungled, well, it doesn't make you feel exactly like king of the hill.

It makes you feel pretty horrible.

And Larry Carson felt pretty horrible.

First Sue, who just didn't want him any more, who seemed to want him less and less every day. Now Nedra who wanted him and took him and then wanted more.

He was, obviously, a failure.

Failure.

He wanted to laugh at the word. Money in the bank, a huge paycheck, a respectable job, a cream-colored Lincoln, all the symbols of suburban status. And what the hell good were all these nice little status symbols to a man who just plain stank in bed?

No good at all.

Obviously.

So where did you go from here?

Away.

Obviously.

Where did you go?

Well, it didn't matter. The only important thing was to get away. You had to either get away from failure or learn to live with it, and there were few things less attractive to the type of man Larry Carson was than learning to live with failure. He just plain didn't *want* to learn to live with failure. It was enough of a problem learning to live with success.

But, if you yourself were the failure, how did you run away? You'd have to run away from yourself, and that seemed a little difficult at first glance. How did a man go about running away from himself?

A good question.

The first step, of course, was just to get away. You couldn't stay around the scene of the failure itself. That would only be rubbing your nose in your own mess, an unpleasant way to spend time.

So you had to get away.

He fumbled for clothing, found it piece by piece, put it on piece by piece. Dressing was a mechanical act and he dressed mechanically, putting his undershorts on inside-out and not even giving a damn, not caring enough to get them right side out. The important thing was just to get dressed and get out, preferably in that order, and that was just what he was doing.

The party was going on around him. It cannot be said that he didn't notice the rest of them. Not noticing them would be something on a par with not noticing a tidal wave, or ignoring an earthquake, or smiling complacently at a typhoon. They were about as noticeable as possible, and, because his eyes still worked and his ears still worked, he sure as hell noticed them.

He just didn't give a damn.

He did not feel excited by what he saw. Nor did he feel disgusted, or even amused.

He simply did not care.

And, when he was dressed, he left. He walked out of the room, carefully shutting the door behind him, and walked down the stairs to the first floor, and went out the front door and shut it quite carefully behind him as well. He paused in front of his car and took a long look at the Forsythe house. It seemed incredibly calm and peaceful, so much so that you could not even tell that a party was going on, much less the type of party he had just left behind him.

Something was wrong with the picture. He felt vaguely that you ought to be able to tell from the street what was going on inside. But you couldn't.

He turned away from the house, got in the driver's side of the cream-colored Lincoln, fitted the key in the ignition and stepped on the gas. After a series of precise maneuvers he was on the Merritt Parkway. He pointed the car toward New York and drove like a well-trained, properly-oiled robot. The speedometer never dipped below fifty miles an hour or rose above sixty-five. He kept the car on the right side of the road and kept his eyes in front of him, thinking very hard about absolutely nothing at all.

Chapter 9

ROZ ROBSHAW MANAGED TO get out of the room.

Not right away, of course. Many things happened before she got out of the room, things that she did not want to think about, things with Steve Gordon and things with one or two other men.

Things like the movie, things invented on the spur of the moment. All manner of things.

Bad things.

Wrong things.

And, when she finally got out of the room with her shoes left behind and her bra left behind and her panties left behind, she did not get out of the house the way Larry Carson had gone. For one thing, Joe had the keys to the car, and Joe was still up in the room with the rest of them, so the only way to get home was to walk, and she didn't have the strength to walk. For another thing, she didn't feel like moving. She felt like sitting by herself in a chair in the Forsythe's living room and thinking painful thoughts.

You're a fine girl, she told herself. You think you're grown up and you think you know a lot about yourself, and then you find out what an infant you are and how little you know of yourself.

You're a fine girl.

You start out happily married to a nice guy who loves you. He's not Mr. Excitement, he's even a little dull, but he loves you and takes good care of you and keeps you happy. He makes nice money and you get whatever you want from him. You don't even have to ask for it. You don't have to ask for anything, because that's the kind of a guy he is. And if he happens to be a little bit on the dull side, at least he doesn't bother you with the things you happen to find dull. He knows you have your own interests and he has his, and he's willing to let you lead your own life.

Soft life, huh? Good spot—every girl should be so lucky. Huh?

Sure.

So you start out this way, and because of a stupid club filled with misfits that neither of you really wanted to get mixed up with in the first place, you find out that men and women can have much deeper relationships than the one you happen to have. You find out that you and Jackson Pierce have a lot in common, and suddenly the soft life you have with Joe doesn't seem so attractive any more. The dullness seems duller and the gap between you seems to loom a little wider, and things start to go bad.

Lousy, huh?

But hold on.

There's more.

You see, you keep going to the lousy parties. And one

night things go absolutely wild, and the sex comes on like a Florida hurricane, and the sad thing is that you find out that you're not really a woman after all, not when the chips are down.

You're an animal.

An animal—no better and no worse than a bitch in heat, a filthy animal with a sexual appetite that's so nauseating you want to vomit. You roll around on the floor with men you don't really know at all and you get hot as a pot-bellied stove with a silly movie on a silly screen, and men get you so hot you can't breathe and it goes on and on and on until you damn near go out of your mind.

So your marriage is falling apart, and your life is falling apart, and you don't love your husband and you hate yourself and there's nothing to do but be an animal, and even that can get dull as dishwater.

So what do you do?

You cry, she answered herself.

And she did. At first the tears wouldn't come, but then they would, and she sat curled up in the chair with nothing under her dress and no shoes on her feet, her eyes flowing over with tears and her body shaking like a leaf and her head aching and ready to split.

And cried.

And cried.

THE NEXT TO LEAVE was Jackson Pierce. He left, not like Larry Carson with blind eyes and not like Roz Robshaw with a heavy heart, but so calmly and dispassionately that it was uncanny. He just got dressed, calmly and efficiently, and walked out. He passed Roz Robshaw in the living room and noticed that she was crying. But he didn't care at all about Roz Robshaw and her tears.

He walked out.

He found his car, got into it and began to drive. He had been sober for a change, almost entirely sober, and the weird sobriety had given him a chance to see things to which alcohol had previously blinded him. He saw himself, on the one hand, and on the other hand he saw all the other people at the party, his wife included, Roz Robshaw included. The vision was clear at first, blurred somewhat when Nedra Marshall had made his flesh overcome his spirit, and even clearer when he had finished with Nedra Marshall and was alone with himself once more.

For years he had thought they were better than he was. For years he was the brawn, the football player who had lucked out and landed a good job while they had to use their brains to get their jobs, the slob who preferred fishing to reading and jazz to Bartok.

To hell with them.

All of them.

They were a bunch of slobs, not him. They lived inside themselves like moles inside the earth, never daring to come up for a breath of fresh air. Hell, fresh air would kill them, the slobs.

He was through with them, through with Eastport, through once and for all with the whole stinking mess. There was a better world, and there were better people, but if he didn't find either it would be all right. He was himself, he knew himself, and everything was going to be all right.

Linda could take herself to hell. That was the first step, to leave her and divorce her and give her as much money as it took to get her off his neck forever. She could have the house, which he hated, and she could have the car, which he also hated—a sprawling ugly house and a sprawling ugly car, the first the product of a homosexual architect with a flair for creative stupidity, the second the product of Detroit's collective understanding of America's collective stupidity.

He would take an apartment in New York, which was more than enough for him, and he would buy a good little Volkswagen, which was also more than enough for him, and then he would tell his illustrative employers to take their job and shove it up their collective anus.

A damned good notion.

He had the money to open up on his own. Public relations was an idiot's game and he could handle it as well as the next slob. He'd been fooling himself—he'd been selling himself short, he knew the game, he could do okay on his own without a bunch of idiots to answer to.

If he went broke, well, that was okay. At least he would be going broke on his own, and the worst thing that could happen would be that he'd have to start all over again, working his tail off and pushing his way uphill until he got to the goddamned top of the heap.

But, eventually, he was going to get to the top. He had one hell of a lot of drive now and he knew it. Nobody could stop him.

It was as though all at once he was making up for all the years of nothingness, for all the wasted time since the day he stepped off the football field and into the gray flannel suit of Midtown Manhattan. Now he was going to make up for lost time. Now he was going to set the goddamned world on its goddamned ear.

He laughed, thinking of all the whiskey he'd swallowed in an attempt to drink himself to death. Whiskey was so unnecessary all at once, so completely useless to him. He could live without whiskey, and he could live without the soft bodies of soft women, and he could live without the suburban sort of security that lulled you to sleep and strangled you while you slept.

He had himself now, and when you have yourself you can live without a lot of things, things that seem indispensable when they are all you have.

He went into his house, packed a bag, drove to the station. He left the car in the station lot, figuring that Linda would find it eventually. When the train came he got on it and let it carry him to New York. On the way he did not waste time relaxing. He spent his time deep in thought, outlining everything in his mind, getting straight on all the mechanics, knowing now what to do and in what order to do it.

It was easy when you had the guts.

That was the trouble with the Eastport people. They just didn't have the guts. They were frightened people, terrified people, disturbed people. They were sick—that was the word he'd been looking for—sick inside with a disease that would eat their souls.

He was healthy.

All along he'd thought that he was sick, that he was no good, that he was a wreck. He'd been wrong, and he'd let himself wallow in self-pity so long that the world was ready to cut him off. He got out just in time.

For a while there he'd thought the Robshaw woman was all right. But she wasn't. She was sick just like the rest of them were sick. It was good to be rid of her, good to be rid of Linda, good to be rid of the lot of them.

When the train hit Grand Central he got out, walking out of the station with the suitcase dangling from his hand like an umbrella. It was a heavy suitcase but he carried it without noticing the weight. He was strong, strong physically and strong mentally. He could swing a heavy suitcase and shoulder heavy responsibilities, and neither sort of weight was capable of getting him down.

He found a medium-priced hotel that would do until he had time to hunt around for an apartment. The hotel was located on the corner of Eighth Avenue and 43rd Street, an old hotel still in good shape with a huge lobby and very high ceilings. He walked into the hotel, through the lobby to the desk and told the sleepy-eyed Negro at the desk that he wanted a room. The clerk passed him the register, thought about asking for cash in advance, then decided after a second look that the man in front of him was not the sort who made it a practice to duck hotel bills.

Jackson Pierce took the pen, signed the book. His signature was firm, authoritative. The clerk nodded and called for a bellhop. Pierce followed the boy to the elevator, rode to his room on the fifth floor, then handed the boy half a dollar.

He left a call at the desk for eight. The next day was Sunday, and he could afford to sleep, but sleeping more than seven hours was a waste of time. And he couldn't afford to waste time.

He showered, then got into bed. His mind was clear and be fell asleep at once.

SUE CARSON WAS IN bad shape. There were black and blue marks all over her thighs and arms. There was a cigarette burn on one breast, and both breasts were raw from the beating they had taken. Her entire body ached over every inch of its surface.

She had never felt better in her life.

She ached all over, inside as well as out. She was not happy, not by any stretch of the imagination. She hated herself for what had been done to her, just as she hated the man who had done the things to her, who had made her body the guinea pig in an experiment of torture and sadism.

Mark Phillips.

Of course, he hadn't been the only one. After all, when a party turns into a full-fledged orgy, you can't limit yourself to one man. There were other men, plenty of them, but in some way they didn't count at all. She submitted to them for two reasons—to soil herself, because she wanted to be soiled, and also because she was in Rome and it was only right to do what the Romans were doing. But it had been no fun.

It was only fun with Mark.

Mark, who hurt her. Mark, who knew her weaknesses so perfectly, so thoroughly, so intimately. Of course it was no cause for wonderment that Mark knew her secrets. They were his secrets as well. She and Mark were a pair, a truly perfect couple of specimens.

He was a sadist. He got his kicks by hurting, by hurting her. Without her pain there would be little or no pleasure in it for him.

And she herself was the opposite number, a masochist. It was all straight out of Krafft-Ebing, a perfect case of a relatively common sexual perversion.

They were quite a pair.

Quite a pair.

Not Abbot and Costello. Not Martin and Lewis. Not

Nichols and May. Not Mutt and Jeff, or Cain and Abel, or ham and eggs.

She hated him, not only because of what he did to her but because of what she was when she was with him. And he no doubt hated her for much the same reasons. The hate they shared made the sex even deeper, harsher, more pleasurable and more terrible.

But they needed each other.

She needed him because she was only alive when he was doing vicious things to her, because she could never feel with anybody else the way she felt when she was with him. And he was the same way—he needed a woman who itched to submit to him.

So there they were.

There was, Sue thought, very little to wish for. Her world was disintegrating quite rapidly, and the world that remained for her was a world of pleasure in pain, a world of sickness and degradation.

Which was not much, but which happened to be all that she had.

THE PARTY DID NOT break up. It disintegrated.

Needless to say, the madcap game of hide-the-keys was not played that night. It was quite unnecessary. No one had the slightest inclination to go home with someone else's husband or wife. As a matter of complete fact, rare was the person who wanted to go home with his or her *own* husband or wife.

Everyone had had about enough.

Bit by bit people broke away and went home. Larry Carson was the first to leave, of course, followed by Roz Robshaw and Jackson Pierce. Roz was soon joined in the living room by her husband, and she and Joe went home together. They did not speak to each other.

One by one, two by two, they trooped out and went home. Finally there were only three of them left.

Walt Forsythe.

And Mary Forsythe.

And, strangely enough, Peggy Phillips.

Because Peggy did not want to go home. She wanted to stay right where she was, wanted to sleep in the arms of Mary Forsythe. It was all right with Mary, who was finding Peggy a rather novel change from men. And it was all right with Walt, who had no desire to interfere in the merry destruction of Peggy Phillips.

So Mary and Peggy went to bed. There was another bed in another room and Walt occupied it.

He did not fall asleep right away. He was tired, exhausted, worn to a frazzle, but he did not fall asleep for hours. First he had to run the course of events through his mind, savoring every memory, thinking about all that he had done and seen and, for that matter, caused.

He was very proud of himself.

He was also very glad that he was still alive. His heart still pumped, his blood still circulated, and God was still being good to him. God or the Devil, whoever was responsible for his soul, had seen fit to grant him a little more time on earth. For this he was extremely grateful.

He lay there, sleepless, and he thought about his heart. It seemed to him as though he were in a strange and very desperate race, a race with time, a race with his own weird and wonderful heart. There was a world full of women, and he had to knock over as many of them as he could before his heart gave out.

And the funny part of it was that each woman he tumbled strained his poor tired heart that much more. It was a spiral, a winding course, and he knew inside that the race he was running was a race he could never win. He listened to his heart, listened to the way it pounded inside his rib cage, and he wondered how many more strains the old heart would take, how many hurdles he would clear before it was all over. Then they would shovel him into a box and drop the box in a hole and cover it with dirt, and then what good would it all be to him? Not much good, he admitted. Not much good at all.

Walt Forsythe lay in bed and listened to his heart, listened to the pounding of it. The sun came up and the room got brighter and still he could not fall asleep.

He listened to his heart and he thought strange thoughts, and gradually he drifted off to sleep in the sunlit room. It was Sunday, Sunday morning. God's day. And just before he drifted off to sleep he heard the slow solemn tolling of church bells.

Chapter 10

FEW PROBLEMS ARE MORE difficult than the one of guessing how various individuals will react to shocks of various magnitudes. Any shock, physical or emotional, has by definition an effect upon the organism subjected to the shock. This is fundamental. What is ticklish is the act of determining how a given person will respond to a given traumatic experience.

For example, you may take two men and shoot each in turn in the stomach with a .32 caliber pistol at relatively close range. One may fall to the floor, clutching himself in an attempt to hold his intestines together. He will pass out, be carted off to the hospital, and, after a period of time, surprise everybody by making a complete recovery and living out his normal lifespan.

The other, however, may ignore the hole in his gut, charge you, get you by the neck, strangle you, take the gun away from you and heave it against the wall.

And then fall down dead.

The same sort of thing will happen on the psychological level. Subject a group of people to a traumatic occurrence and watch what happens. Some of them will crumple up like the first gunshot victim, utterly destroyed, only to recover miraculously and go through life with an apparently undamaged psyche. The experience, if anything, seems to have toughened them. Their defenses are stronger, their minds work more precisely, and they are far less likely to get figuratively shot in the stomach in the future.

Others will appear to weather the blow. Then, suddenly or gradually, they will begin to fall apart.

The party at the home of Walter and Mary Forsythe is a case in point. By all rules it came as a shock to the people who attended. In various degrees, everybody there was moved in one direction or the other. Some crumpled at once. Others crumpled slowly. Some seemed quite unmoved by the entire course of events.

Yet the party was nothing if it was not traumatic. It had its effects for better and for worse, and no one who attended it remained untouched by it. This would have been quite impossible—a psychological version of getting shot in the stomach and having the bullet bounce off you. Things simply do not happen that way. You live or you die, but either way you have a hole in your stomach.

SUNDAY WAS A SLOW day. It was, of course, a period of recuperation, of wound-licking, of planning and plotting and adjusting. It was very fortunate that no one had a job to go to, that the children did not have to be driven to and from school, that meals were not to be cooked or dishes to be washed.

Instead, people remained in bed as long as possible, took long baths in warm tubs, drank more or less moderately, and sank restfully and a bit gratefully into the soothing monotony of television. Television, the least pleasant product of contemporary technology with the possible exception of the hydrogen bomb, does have its uses. Even an intelligent person has to admit as much. The unbelievably vile tripe served up hour after hour and night after night has a markedly beneficial effect upon a person loaded down with worries. It takes his mind off his worries and centers it upon nothing more consequential than whether some joker will win a fortune, whether the cowboys will catch the Indian, whether the teenaged idiot of a rock 'n' roll singer will ever hit the right note.

So they watched television, and drank more or less moderately, and took long baths, and went to bed early. Sunday was the beginning of what might be called the healing process. It started it, and Monday helped it along. Just as Sunday provided methodical relaxation, Monday provided methodical absorption in meaningless tasks. The routine of work had its own sort of therapeutic value, and by the time work was over and Monday night dinner was on the table, things were a good deal better all the way around.

Or, if they were not really any better, they were at least a good deal easier to take.

The week itself was something very different to each person involved. For the Forsythes, for example, it wasn't too different from a good many other weeks. They had both been through the same sort of thing frequently in the course of their life together. They knew each other and they knew themselves, and in a sense they were as well adjusted as most people—sick, of course, but adjusted to their sickness. The key point of any therapy for a neurosis is not the cure of the neurosis but the object of bringing the neurotic to the point where he can learn to live with his idiosyncrasy. Walt and Mary knew what was wrong with them and were happy as they were.

So they went on. Walt worked, sporadically, and Mary took care of the house, sporadically, and in the evenings they sat and talked and, occasionally, made love. They talked about the party, and about the people, and about the movie, which they ran off again one night and which set them off on a rather intense bout of lovemaking. All in all, they simply continued to live their life.

Steve and Nancy Gordon also appeared relatively untouched by what they had gone through. Steve had spent most of the party with Roz Robshaw, and while she was certainly touched by the situation, he himself seemed relatively secure. Nancy had started the night with Mark Phillips, but luckily he had quickly disposed of her and gone off with Sue Carson. Then Nancy drifted to Walt Forsythe, and although what they had done might have been classified as bizarre, she had enjoyed all of it immensely.

The Marshalls also came through it alive. At first it was

rough for both of them, with a good deal of insecurity and fear on both sides. They spoke infrequently during the days and slept on separate sides of their double bed during the nights, neither of them quite daring to make a move toward the other.

On Thursday things relaxed tremendously. They began to talk, guardedly at first and then more openly, until they were able to see the party for what it was to them, a deep plunge into forbidden waters from which they had very luckily been able to swim to shore. Now they were on dry land, and still very much in love, and they knew for certain that they no longer needed the stimulation of other flesh in order to keep their marriage alive.

They also decided that Eastport was another stimulation which they did not need. A short time thereafter they moved back to Manhattan. Don looked around and managed to find a livable apartment on West 46th Street near Ninth Avenue. It was a fourth floor walkup in a less-than-perfect neighborhood, but the low rental was attractive. They had to save their capital so that Don could get started as a writer. He quit his job you see, and began writing for a living.

In time he produced books, and his wife produced children, and eventually the apartment on 46th Street was too small. But they did not move to the suburbs. They took a flat in Canarsie, remaining within New York City limits, staying away from the insanity of Connecticut which had started by threatening their marriage and which ended by driving them closer and closer together.

They became, in short, an ideal married couple. And, as a result, we may dismiss them now and refer to them no more. Ideal married couples do not make for interesting reading, as we know, and as Don Marshall himself grew to realize when he wrote his own books.

BILL AND PIDGE JANSEN did not have it quite so easy. Bill and Pidge Jansen did not have it easy at all, as a matter of fact, and if you said that they had it pretty rotten you might not be far from the truth.

It took Bill a long time to realize that he was not an image on a screen. The delusion, mildly hysterical in retrospect, was incredibly real at the time. And when he realized that he had not been on a screen he took a long look at what he had been doing, and at what his wife had been doing, and quietly popped his cork.

So did Pidge. She had always been on the borderline of hysteria and had now slipped over the edge. As a result, the two of them spent several days shouting at one another at the very top of their young lungs. Once Pidge threw the greater part of a set of dishes at her husband, hitting him about once in five shots, and once Bill got quite upset and hit her on the head with a frying pan, knocking her thoroughly unconscious, stripping off her clothing and raping her while she was out cold. This, incidentally, may well have been the only way in the world to rape Pidge. If she had not been unconscious she could never have been capable of refusing.

After that delightful little occurrence things at least took on the semblance of normalcy. A psychiatrist would have undoubtedly pronounced both of them insane, but they presented a sane exterior to the world and managed to live through a good many things. They lived through Thursday, for example, and they lived through Friday, although both days they would lapse into deep silences and go into strange talking jags.

Friday night Bill got a phone call. It was from Walt Forsythe, and the message was that there was to be a meeting that Saturday night. Meetings were normally two weeks apart, but Forsythe had decided unilaterally that once every two weeks was not frequent enough. Bill agreed with him, and so did Pidge, and they agreed to go. Forsythe also decreed that his house would be the permanent meeting-place, because the sound-proofed room was so convenient, and again Bill and Pidge were with him all the way.

The thought of the meeting the following night excited them both so much that they spent the evening making love. They were very good at it.

They did it several times.

WHEN WALT FORSYTHE CALLED Joe Robshaw, explaining the purpose of the call, Joe told him he'd let him know.

He went into the living room where Roz was reading and explained what Forsythe had had to say.

"Well," she said. "Of course you told him we would come."

"I told him I'd let him know."

"Really? Call him and tell him we're coming."

Joe picked up his pipe, tamped tobacco into the bowl and lit it. "You can go if you want to," he said. "I don't feel like going."

"You don't?"

He shook his head.

"I suppose you're not an animal like the rest of us. I suppose you're a nice puritanical soul. Straight-laced and pure. Not the type to go down to the pigsty with the rest of the animals. Might get your clothes soiled. Is that the general idea?"

"No."

"Well, what is it?"

"I just don't want to."

"No reason?"

He took a breath. released it. "I just don't think I'd enjoy it, Roz. I'd rather sit home."

"That's exciting," she said. "Sitting home."

"You can go if you want to."

"A fine marriage," she said. "We're supposed to share things, Joe. We're supposed to do things together. But jolly Joseph says I can go and that's the end of it."

"Roz—"

"You don't think you'd like it, huh? The way you didn't like it with Ned Marshall? I saw you with her, Joe. I saw you going to her like an animal. She finished with one and was ready for another, and you went to her while she smelled to high heaven of another man. That's my Puritan husband, isn't it?"

"Damn you, Roz!"

She smiled. It was not a pretty smile. "You like it," she said. "And I like it. Because you're an animal and I'm an animal. We're animals, not people. And it's a damned good thing we're both animals because it's the only damn thing we have in common!"

He walked to the phone. He held the receiver to his ear and dialed a number. The phone rang three times before it was answered.

"Walt," he said slowly, "this is Joe. Joe Robshaw . . . Look, I asked Roz and she thinks it's a good idea. I mean about having the meetings more often, and at your house . . . that's right. I think so too . . . Right, Walt. We'll be there about nine."

After Forsythe had hung up, Joe Robshaw stood for a long moment looking at the phone in his hand. Slowly, barely aware of what he was doing, he placed the receiver in the cradle. Then he went back to the living room and sat down.

He reached for his pipe. It had gone out and he had to

light it again. Then he picked up the evening paper, the late edition of the *Telegram*, and went over the closing prices on the Toronto exchange. There was a mining stock listed that he'd been watching. It looked as though it might be time to buy.

PEGGY PHILLIPS WAS A model wife. She was more considerate than ever of both her husband and their children. The meals were ready on time, the clothes got washed, the beds got made. And she was always pleasant, never flaring up, never running away and bursting into tears when one of the kids got to be just too much to take.

But, she thought, it was very strange. She was doing all of this on the surface, but while she did these things it was as though she was walking around while still asleep. She felt nothing, ever. That was why she could act so smoothly, so easily.

It was very simple. All you had to do was close your eyes on the inside, so that you didn't feel or see or hear anything that was happening to you.

And you waited.

Not for Mary Forsythe. She had enjoyed making love with Mary, there was no getting around that, but she couldn't help knowing that for Mary lesbianism was only a pleasant diversion, a game to occupy time and change the scene between heterosexual encounters. Mary was good to her, Mary was good for her, Mary was wonderful to make love to and equally wonderful to be made love to by. But falling in love with Mary was obviously out of the question.

And Peggy Phillips needed somebody to love.

Not Mark, of course. Mark was around, but Mark was no more interested in her than she was in him. Mark, too, had changed, and Peggy was not certain what the change was and was fairly confident that she didn't want to know any more about it. Mark was sick, he ought to see an analyst, there was something wrong with him, but why should she care, what did it matter to her, because some day soon, God help her, she was getting out, getting out and away once and for all.

Someday soon.

That was the plan. That was why she could go on, day after day, making the beds and doing the dishes and cooking the meals, keeping the house nice and talking nice to the kids and staying out of Mark's way when he was in one of his moods, which was rather often lately. Because all of this was just something she had to live through until something better came along.

Which would be soon.

Soon she would leave. Up and out and away, away to somewhere where the gay girls lived, where she would find somebody to love, somebody who couldn't bear the touch of a man, somebody to hold her close all night long and say *I love you, Peggy*, and really mean every last word of it, somebody to be with twenty-four hours a day, seven days a week, fifty-two weeks a year.

In the meanwhile, there was Mary. There was Mary for sexual pleasure, for the release of tension, for a little more excitement and a little less boredom. In the meanwhile there was Mary, once every two weeks until finally she got up her nerve and straightened up and flew right, right away, away and free.

Wheeee!

And when Mary called her, telling her about the meeting a week ahead of time, there had been a lot more excitement and a lot less boredom. And of course she had checked first with Mark, and of course Mark had been all for it— what the hell, he certainly wasn't getting anything from *her* and all any man cared about was how much he was getting, that was the way every last one of them was—so she had told Mary they would be coming, and Mary had been glad.

Then she had asked Mary the question, whether the two of them could do it again, and Mary had said that the program was going to be changed. There were no movies this time, Mary explained. The entertainment was going to be supplied by the participants. So if Peggy didn't mind doing it on a stage with everybody watching, well, then, it was all right with Mary.

Peggy thought about it. She minded, of course. Anyone who *didn't* mind would be on a par with Mary. But she told herself that she would do it the same way she did the dishes and made the beds and washed the clothes and cooked the meals. She would do it without feeling the watching eyes, the dirty words, the heavy breathing of the audience, without, in fact, feeling anything at all.

Anything, that is, but Mary.

And that struck her as funny, and she started to giggle uncontrollably. Then she calmed down, and told Mary that was certainly aces with her, and then she put down the receiver and started to laugh again, louder this time.

Chapter 11

SUE CARSON LIVED ALONE now. Larry had never called her and she did not know what had become of him. We know, of course, but we will get to that later on. In the meantime let's concern ourselves with Sue, who likes to be hurt.

Like Peggy, she lived in a shell. A very hard and opaque shell. She, too, had a special way of enjoying sex, and without that way she could not properly enjoy life.

So she was very pleased when Mary called.

And she did not mind Mary's suggestion at all. The suggestion that she and Mark put on a special show for the rest of the people.

It sounded fine.

Because she wouldn't like it. It was bad enough being beaten, more than bad, but it would be infinitely worse with everybody watching her and knowing what was wrong with her. That would be horrible.

Which, of course, meant that it would be very good indeed,

The humiliation, she knew instinctively, would add to her enjoyment. It would add immeasurably, as a matter of fact.

The mental picture of Mark making love to her in the ways that Mark alone made love, with everybody else doing nothing but watching, was such a supremely exciting thing that she was trembling.

And, simultaneously, such a frightening picture that she was terrified.

So, alone in her big house, Sue Carson shook with desire and fear. She couldn't wait for Saturday, and at the same time she wished fervently that Saturday would never come.

It was hard getting to sleep that night. She watched television until the late late show went off the air, watched the five nauseating minutes of meditation that followed the late late show, and when she was alone with the test pattern, still she did not feel much like going to sleep.

She took a sleeping pill.

And, after she had swallowed the sleeping pill, she thought what a good idea it might be to take all the other sleeping pills, to toss them down her throat one after the other, to keep on taking them until there were no more left to take.

And then to sleep. A long sleep, a good sleep, a deep sleep.

One from which she would not wake up.

She put the pills in the medicine chest. She went to bed, and after a very long time she slept.

LIKE SUE CARSON, LINDA Pierce was alone. Jackson was gone. But unlike Sue Carson, Linda Pierce had heard from her husband. She had agreed instantly to the divorce terms he had set, had signed the paper from the Mexican attorney living in New York, and had taken the money and house Jackson had so graciously settled on her.

She still didn't quite believe him. It was hardly like Jackson to do *anything* which was quite that forceful. Jackson simply was not a forceful man. He was, if anything, the utter opposite.

Linda wasn't sure whether or not she liked the idea. It was nice having all that money without having Jackson around. It was just plain nice not having Jackson around, as far as that went.

But *he* had left *her*. And that part wasn't so nice. Men did not leave Linda. She left them, and that was the way it was supposed to be.

But she wasn't letting herself get all upset about it. She was, instead, getting as much mileage as she could out of the week. The party had liberated some element or other in everybody present, and the element it had liberated in Linda was the one commonly known as nymphomania.

She could not get enough.

Unlike everybody else, Linda was not waiting for the party. Let *them* wait, and the hell with them. She was busy making up for lost time.

Not that she'd lost *that* much time, but it certainly did look that way the way she was making up for it. Any man who came near her that week wound up coming a lot closer to her than he'd planned to. It was not safe for a man to ring the doorbell of the Pierce home. Linda would answer the door, and Linda would drag the man inside, and Linda would be wearing a housecoat with nothing under it, and the house coat would keep slipping open, and pretty soon the housecoat would come off, and then and there the man would be with Linda.

And pretty soon the man's clothes would be off, too, and they would be in the bedroom, and the man would be getting the ride of his life. He would have beautiful breasts to cushion him and beautiful thighs to hug him and a beautiful mouth to whisper passion words in his ear. There was something else that was quite attractive as well, and it came into play, and it was utilized with incredible dexterity.

A few men learned not to go near the Pierce house. Other men, more adventurous, learned that it was a lot of fun at Linda's little home. Linda Pierce had invented, or rediscovered, one goddamned gas of a mouse trap.

And the world beat a path to her door.

She took on everybody. There was a delivery boy from the corner drugstore with some rather intimate medicine that she had phoned out for. He expected a tip, but the tip which he got was quite a bit more than he expected. He had never had a woman before, and Linda Pierce found this a rather startling notion. So he got a woman and he got quite a bit of a woman, and by the time she let him go he was too tired to peddle his bicycle back to the store.

There was the mailman, and there was the milkman, and there was a whole slew of door-to-door salesmen, and there was a neighbor paying a visit, and there were . . . well, there were quite a few men.

She would do anything and everything. Many prostitutes have certain scruples, certain acts they will not perform, but Linda Pierce was not a prostitute.

And she had no scruples.

When Mary phoned her, she said that she would be delighted to come. She thought that it would be quite a bit of fun, and she had decided to have all the fun she could out of life.

And fun meant only one thing.

THERE ARE TWO LEFT, and they give perhaps the clearest indication of the maxim, that two persons could react quite differently to the same phenomenon.

The two are, of course, Jackson Pierce and Larry Carson. They have a lot in common. Both are successful, and both have left their wives.

And there the similarity ends.

But completely.

Jackson Pierce devoted the week to building a new life. Somewhere along the line he managed to eliminate the old. He found a Mexican lawyer who specialized in quickie divorces, put a little pressure on to make it as quickie a divorce as possible, took a day off and flew down to Chihuahua. He came back not too many hours later without a wife. It was that simple.

Everything, it turned out, was equally simple. He called up his employers and told them he was ceasing to be one of their employees. They were surprised, in that they had expected they would be the ones to terminate the employment. In this respect they were quite like Linda. Neither were particularly sorry to see the end of Jackson, yet both felt hurt that it had been his decision and not theirs.

Because Jackson Pierce began to work like a dynamo, and like a very high-powered dynamo at that. Inside of a week he had talked his way into two very good accounts. Inside of a month he had four more very good accounts, all of them very satisfied with the marvelous job he was doing for them, plus an apartment in the west seventies and an office on Fifth Avenue at 47th Street.

Inside of a year he could afford better than an apartment on West 73rd Street, because by then he employed twelve people, made close to forty thousand a year, saved money, invested it properly, stayed off the sauces, and generally did his best to make the very best sort of life possible for himself. Which was a very good life indeed.

The secret, if there was one, lay in the fact that he refused to let up. No matter what happened, Pierce kept going. He worked twenty hours a day on a good day and no less than ten on a bad one. He worked efficiently. He did not stop to daydream and he did not stop to feel sorry for himself. When anything got in his way, he had one unfailing remedy.

He worked harder.

And it worked for him.

The money came in. He made the right deals, the shrewd deals, until one morning he woke up and discovered that he had an absolute boat-load of money. He could sell the agency and retire, still young.

But he didn't want to retire. Work was everything, the only relaxation after work was more work, and none of the women he had bothered with had been worth more than a one-night stand to him.

But the agency didn't make any sense. The money it brought in was heavy money, but he already had enough money, more than enough money.

Then things happened. For one thing, he met the perfect girl. She was the perfect girl in every respect, so perfect that he married her first and then slept with her, and he and the girl went out into the wilds of Maine and bought a children's camp. It was a run-down children's camp, and it was not making any money, and they bought it because they both had strong ideas about what a children's camp should be like, and as far as they knew there were no camps run along the lines they had in mind.

The children's camp did not make any money. It was not designed to make any money. But it made a lot of children happy, and it also made Jackson and Marilyn Pierce happy.

Which was why they bought it in the first place.

IF JACKSON PIERCE WENT steadily up, Larry Carson went steadily down.

His story is easy to tell. It is the story of the compulsive drinker, and this story is one that is familiar to almost everybody. It went by stages, and the stages started with Scotch and went all the way down the line to muscatel, and from there to kerosene and wood alcohol and hair tonic and shoe polish.

Larry Carson wound up on the Bowery.

The beard went, somewhere along the way, and the flip manner went, somewhere along the way, and all that was left in time was a man named Larry who did not have a last name, a man who lived in Narragansett House on the corner of Bowery and Grand, a man who drank whatever he could find and talked at night about a strange and frightening party.

The story of the party was a good story. It was very sexy, and the men who knew Larry liked a good sexy story. They didn't mind hearing it over and over.

Of course they did not believe it. It was not the sort of story you believe, not when you are a bum on the Bowery with both feet in the gutter and wine on your brain. It was an obvious fabrication, but there was a tolerance prevalent in that particular area which kept anyone from questioning a word Larry said.

They did not believe him, but they accepted him. If he

wanted to tell a sexy story and pretend it was true, well, that was his business.

And pass the wine, will you?

YOU MAY NOW FORGET all about Larry Carson and Jackson Pierce, just as you have forgotten all about Don and Nedra Marshall. They have found themselves, they have levelled off to their own particular levels, and they are no longer interesting. When a person becomes predictable, that person is no longer an asset to a book. We know that Don and Ned will live healthy lives, and we know that Jackson will be happy, and we know that Larry will drink himself to death. This much we know.

So to hell with them.

We have other things to consider now. We have to consider our group, and our poor group has dwindled in size. Some of the charter members have disappeared. They are gone, and the group must go on without them:

The Gordons are still with us, Nancy and Steve. So are Walt and Mary Forsythe, and Joe and Roz Robshaw. So too are Bill and Pidge Jansen, and Mark and Peggy Phillips. Sue Carson is here, and Linda Pierce is here.

That is all.

And now it is Saturday night, and time for the festivities to get under way. The scene is the Forsythe home, the permanent scene according to all signs. The time is a little after eight and the guests have not yet begun to arrive.

Walt Forsythe is in the living room at the bar. He is wearing a white dinner jacket and a pair of black worsted trousers. He loves to dress up, and this seems to be a good opportunity.

He is preparing drinks.

His wife is in the kitchen, fooling around with a tray of hors d'oeuvres, putting little dabs of pimento on top of little crackers spread with a cheese dip. She is careful to place a piece of pimento in the precise center of each cracker.

There is something symbolic about the act which appeals to her.

It is almost time. Soon the guests will arrive, and then they will drink their perfunctory drinks and chatter their perfunctory chatter until it is time. When it is time Walt will lead the parade upstairs and close the big door.

And it will begin.

Get ready, everybody. It is Saturday night. Saturday night in the tottering town of Eastport, and we are going to a party.

It'll be a ball.

Chapter 12

THE DOORBELL AT THE Forsythe house rang before Mary Forsythe had finished placing a single piece of pimento on the last several crackers. She heard the chimes peal melodically, looked regretfully at the tray of canapés, and called to Walt, asking him if he would be good enough to answer the door.

Walt was good enough. He put the lid on the ice bucket, walked to the door, and opened it to admit Linda Pierce. He smiled, and she smiled, and she came inside and he closed the door.

"You're looking good," he said. She was—she wore a black sheath that hugged her figure like a second skin, the hem around her knees, the neckline plunging halfway to her navel. The dress left very little to the imagination. The little that wasn't visible was more than suggested by the taut fabric.

"Thank you, kind sir. You look all right yourself. Is that a uniform?"

"Just a dinner jacket."

She faked a curtsey. "A noble dinner jacket," she said. "A very noble dinner jacket indeed. And what have we here?"

Her hand darted, touching Walter Forsythe in a most intimate place. "My," she exclaimed. "I detect a certain amount of interest. A three-dimensional exhibition of delicious masculine distress. You shouldn't let such an exhibition go to waste, kind sir. If you would be of a mind of repairing to the couch—"

"Now now, Linda."

She pouted.

"Not that I wouldn't like to," he said, "but you have to remember the rules. The rest of the guests will be arriving shortly. In the meantime—"

"In the meantime," she cut in, the pose dropped for the moment, "in the meantime, I feel like getting a boffing. A real rousing boffing. I feel like giving you a ride you won't forget."

"There will be plenty of time."

Her eyes hardened. "There's never time enough. They told me the same thing when I was at school at Clifton— take your time, plenty of time, just relax and take your time. But there isn't time to do everything you want to do. And you know what I want to do?"

"I know."

"I want to get boffed," she said. "That's what I want to do. You see these?"

She touched her breasts.

"Best pair in the country," she told him. "That's what everybody says. Not just one little girl's opinion. Wouldn't you like to fool around with them a little?"

"Later—"

"Later!" She stamped her foot, and Forsythe thought that she looked like nothing more than a petulant little child—rather a well-built child, but a child nevertheless with a child's mind and a child's soul in a woman's body. This, of course, was her particular form of escape. She retreated into immaturity, made sex a toy and played night and day.

He found her quite interesting.

"Come here," he said, taking her arm. "Let me fix you a drink."

"I don't want a drink."

"Of course you do," he said. He poured a martini from the shaker and handed it to her. "Just drink your drink," he told her, "and pretty soon the others will get here and the party will start."

"Good," she said, softly. "I like parties. They're fun."

BY THE TIME THE Gordons came, Mary had finished putting pieces of pimento on top of all the crackers. She answered the door this time, the tray in her hand and a smile on her face. "Steve," she said, "and Nancy. Come on in, have a canapé. Walt'll fix you both a drink. I'm so glad you could come."

Steve and Nancy Gordon wandered slowly about the room, sipping their drinks, munching the rather tasteless cheese-dip concoctions, waiting for something to happen.

It didn't take long for Linda to swing into action, and Steve wasn't quite as reluctant to oblige as Walt had been. They settled themselves down on the couch and began the rather enjoyable game of seeing how excited each could get the other. Both, of them did quite well, but Steve discovered in a short time that she had the edge. She had the shortest fuse of any broad he had ever come across. All he had to do was slip her a quick feel and she was climbing the walls. It was really something.

"That's right," she told him. "Keep your hand there. Keep doing that. God, that feels good. You have no idea how good that feels. Oooh, don't stop, don't ever stop, I'll kill you if you stop. Ooooooooh!"

And all he was doing, Steve thought to himself, was slipping her a little feel. He had his hand inside the plunging neckline and his fingers were wrapped around the sweetest and biggest boob with which he'd ever come in contact. And every time he gave the stiff little nipple a pinch she went into orbit.

"Put your other hand here. That's right. Higher up, all the way up, that's right. That's good, Steve. That's very good, it feels so nice, God, I love it, Steve, I love it so much!"

He did what she wanted him to do. It was beginning to get to him now and he wanted to get things started with a bang instead of waiting for the others to arrive. He forced himself to wait, knowing that the longer he put it off the better it was going to be when it finally got going.

And it was going to be good. It was going to be very good with her. She was there to please and he was going to let her please him. Hell, he knew what they were saying about her. The word was out—she was putting out for the world, and both she and the world were getting one hell of a charge out of it.

An image occurred to him. She was a huge delectable cake, the pride of the bakery.

And he was going to make a pig of himself. He was going to cut himself a real big piece.

WALT WAS ON HAND to greet Sue Carson, the next arrival. He flashed her a huge smile which she did not return. Instead the little girl looked up at him, her eyes troubled but eager.

"Is Mark here yet?" she wanted to know. "He said he was coming. Is he here yet?"

"He should get here soon."

"Oh," she said. "Well. That's good."

She turned down both a drink and a cracker and found a chair for herself off in a corner. The others said hello to her but she acted as if she didn't see or hear them. She sat by herself, hands folded in her lap like a penitent schoolgirl being kept after class.

Again, Walt Forsythe was amused. Two more had found their element—Sue Carson and Mark Phillips. The masochist and the sadist. He grinned, remembering the old story about the masochist, shouting *Beat me Hurt me Whip me*, and the sadist sayings imply, *No*.

But that wasn't the way it was with Mark and Sue, not at all. She would scream to be beaten and he would wale the tar out of her. Walt smiled, wondering how the spectacle would go over with the rest of them when it was performed on stage. Their reaction would be interesting to note. All reactions were becoming very interesting, and Walt had to admit that the club was more than living up to expectations. If only it could go on forever. If only it could keep getting better and better, or worse and worse, depending upon one's point of view.

If only his heart would take it—

The thought sobered him and he went to the bar to build himself a drink. He leaned against a wall, resplendent in his white dinner jacket, playing host and waiting for the rest of them to arrive.

And arrive they did.

Next the Jansens. Pidge and Bill. Walt noticed the anticipation in Sue Carson's eyes when the bell rang, then watched it fade and die when Mary opened the door and the Jansens came in. They came in, took drinks, and looked around the room for partners.

Bill latched onto Sue Carson first, then got the obvious message that she couldn't be less interested. Without losing step he picked up on Nancy Gordon and guided her to a chair. He sat down and she settled in his lap.

"We've got to put on a show for the people," he told her. "Got to keep it interesting. Otherwise they won't pay us."

Nancy Gordon didn't seem to understand. But she did understand the way Bill was kissing her, and she did understand the way he was touching her, and the idiotic words he was whispering in her ear became a little less important the more he kissed and stroked her.

Pidge Jansen had looked around the room for a man. Since Walt was the only one available, it wasn't long before she was nestled in his arms with her hot body pressed up against him.

And she, too, had things to say.

"Put on an act," she told him. "Even if you don't like it, pretend you like it. Even if you don't like me, you have to make pretend."

"Why?"

"Otherwise," she explained very intently, "I will feel bad. I will be hurt, hurt without a flirt and feel like dirt, a hurt little skirt with an alert quirt. So just pretend, and bend and wend and send. Just make believe, don't grieve."

She was cracking up. He saw the symptoms—the rhyming speech, the weird flashes of perception that accompanied the complete loss of touch with reality. Pidge Jansen was showing symptoms of schizophrenia. She was in the process of going quietly mad.

And the interesting thing, Walt thought to himself, was that Bill himself was breaking down at the same time, unable to distinguish between the real and the imaginary, still thinking he was on a stage or a screen or that he was just an image in the mind of another person. An interesting delusion. Walt wondered what particular form of psychotic behavior it represented, and wondered at the same time just how long it would be before the pair of them were carted off to a sanitarium.

Then he stopped wondering, because he had more important things to do than wonder. Pidge Jansen was so close to him that every detail of her lush body pressed into him, and he let his mind go clear and surrendered himself to her, plunging his tongue deep into her mouth, cupping her hard buttocks with his big hands and pressing her close to him.

One thought flashed through his mind. If this is madness, he thought, make the most of it.

JOE AND ROZ ROBSHAW and Mark and Peggy Phillips arrived about the same time. There, however, the similarity between the two couples ended. Mark and Peggy were both people with missions. Mark at once went to Sue and Peggy just as promptly went to Mary. Mark and Sue merely sat together, waiting for something to happen, but Peggy forced herself upon Mary right away. She began kissing the older woman right there in the middle of the living room with everybody watching, her arms tight around Mary's back, her breasts pressed against Mary's larger breasts, her hot tongue in Mary's hot mouth.

The Robshaws were at the opposite extreme. They separated the minute they entered the Forsythe house. Each took a drink and found a chair. Neither Joe nor Roz made any attempt at conversation, seeming satisfied to sip their drinks slowly and to gaze around the room with expressions of dispassionate gloom.

The two presented a startling contrast in themselves. Roz, always a quiet dresser, was decked out as though she was trying to buck Linda Pierce for the Slut of the Year trophy. Her sweater was white as snow and absolutely skin-tight. Her slacks were black as sin and, if possible, even tighter. On her feet she wore black leather sandals that were slabs of leather held to her feet by thongs. Her toes showed, and the nails were painted a rather bizarre scarlet.

Joe, on the other hand, was always a model of neatness—nothing flashy, but not a hair out of place. Today all the hairs were out of place. His brown tweed suit was badly rumpled, his shirt was soiled around the collar, and he needed a shave. He looked as though he'd been needing the same shave for the past several days.

Interesting, Walt thought. Very interesting. Disintegration by guilt, repression of almost everything.

Very interesting. Roz, when she fell apart, played the slut. Joe, when he fell apart, discarded the role of Wall Street broker and let himself fall apart at the seams. But he knew instinctively that the Robshaws still had a long way to fall, a long drop before they hit what would be the end of their particular line.

It would be interesting to watch them fall.

Interesting.

He seized upon the word, turning it over and over in his mind. Participation was pleasant, observation was interesting—that seemed to be the way it went. Well, tonight would be both—exciting, because the participation would be more than adequate; interesting, because observation would be quite rewarding.

He held Pidge close and surveyed the room rapidly. Steve Gordon and Linda Pierce were still playing hot games on the couch while Bill Jansen and Nancy Gordon played equally warm games in a chair. Peggy and Mary continued their embrace while Mark and Sue continued to stare meaningfully into each other's eyes. And the Robshaws kept their weird vigil, drank their drinks and stared their morbid stares.

The stage was set.

Walt gently pushed Pidge aside, then deposited his empty glass on the bar. "Show time," he called out, assuming the air of a gallant leader. "Everybody up and at 'em. Let's get this show on the road."

He led the way, with Pidge clinging to his arm like a leech, led them up the staircase to the special room on the second floor. And, one by one or two by two, they followed him.

He opened the door, flicked a switch on the wall, stepped aside to let them in and closed the door after them.

The door clicked shut and he turned a lock to make sure they would not be disturbed. A disturbance from the outside world was certainly the last thing they needed.

Then he turned to face the group. He looked at them, watched the way they surveyed the room with various expressions on various faces. No two people reacted in quite the same manner to the display confronting them. It seemed to excite some while revolting others, and Walt was amused.

The stage was set.

Chapter 13

THE ROOM WAS A study. A thick wine-colored carpet ran from wall-to-wall, broken up this time by small intimate mattresses instead of the pillows which had served as seats a week ago. The mattresses were covered with a sort of robin's-egg-blue material that contrasted quite violently with the red carpet. The walls had been painted a flat black, further complicating and intensifying the color scheme.

But the colors were the least of it. Where a week ago there had been a motion picture screen, there was now quite literally a stage. One entire section at the front of the room had been raised approximately eighteen inches, and the resultant stage was carpeted in canary yellow and was dominated by a mammoth bed.

The message was obvious. The mattresses on the floor were the seats for the audience. The bed on the stage was a plush area for performers. The whole room was permeated with an air of decadence and depravity, a feel of public sex and private perversion.

Walt walked to the front of the room, mounted the stage and turned to survey the audience. Quickly if somewhat theatrically he gave them their instruction. The evening, he explained, was to be devoted to instruction and practice in various modes of physical love. Each person was to select one of the mattresses and occupy it alone. Then he would summon individuals to the stage, the house lights would go down, the spotlight would focus on the performers, and the demonstrations would take place.

First, though, everyone was kindly requested to remove his or her clothing. When this was accomplished, the men and women selected individual mattresses and sat down upon them. Walt, on stage, removed his own clothing, standing before them naked except for the smile on his face. The smile widened.

"Our first performers," he announced, "will be Peggy Phillips and Mary Forsythe. I'm certain the show they put on will be well received by each and every one of you. They've gone to a good deal of trouble rehearsing this particular act—" a wink here "—and I hope we'll all enjoy it as much as they do."

Walt stepped down, flicked a switch that darkened the room, flicked another switch that bathed the bed onstage in a yellow glow. Then he found an unoccupied mattress and took a seat.

Mary Forsythe was the first to reach the stage. She walked briskly, confidently, her stride firm and her arms swinging freely at her sides. She was naked, of course, and her breasts looked huge in the yellow light.

Peggy joined her, but Peggy did not share her confidence. The smaller girl walked slowly, almost reluctantly, her eyes downcast and her hands knotted into tiny fists. It would be all right, she told herself. The sexual release was all that would matter, the rest would be unimportant, she would go through the paces and submit to the stares like a sleepwalker, like a flickering image in a shady dream.

Because soon it would not matter, soon nothing would matter.

Soon she would be in New York, away from all of this, away from all these people who raped her young body with their hot and evil eyes. She would be with a girl, and she would love the girl, and that was all that would matter.

She watched as Mary sat down on the edge of the bed. She let her eyes run over Mary's body, and suddenly the audience was forgotten. All she could see was Mary, all that mattered was Mary.

That was enough.

Pidge Jansen watched the two women kissing. It looked very nice, she thought. Nice, mice, spice. She noticed the way Peggy's breasts pressed against Mary's breasts and thought the spectacle was very interesting. It was all done so neatly, with Mary's nipples pressing tight against Peggy's nipples. Tits wits with pits, she thought. Boobies with rubies. Gobs of knobs.

The more the two women found to do to each other, the more Pigeon became absorbed in what they were doing. Rhyming words flashed through her mind, weird sensations flooded over her soft skin, and her eyes kept up their constant vigil of the epic unfolding on the little stage.

Stage rage wage cage. A stage in a cage and a cage on a stage.

Her breasts itched and her tummy itched and she did not want to watch any more. She wanted to go on the prowl.

Prowl, growl, prowl and howl. Howl was a poem. Best minds of my generation destroyed by madness, starving, hysterical, naked. What was becoming of all those best minds? Why was everybody naked? Or starving, or hysterical, or clerical, or merrical, or—

She crawled on her hands and knees, crawled like an animal with her breasts hanging straight down and her thighs rubbing together as she moved. She crawled directly to the mattress where Roz Robshaw was sitting.

"Roz—"

"Oh. What is it?"

"What they're doing—" *Doing, bluing, cooing, wooing.*

"Well?"

"Let's do it, Roz." *Do it, knew it, me-too it, woo it, me-it and you it.*

"But—"

"Oh, please! Roz, you don't have to do anything. Just lie there, lie there in the sky there and die there. I mean, just stretch out, I mean—"

"I—"

"I want to, Roz. I never tried it, Roz. How do we know we don't like it if we don't try it?"

"But—"

Pigeon's eyes rolled. "You've got to humor me, Roz. They call me Pigeon but my name is Helena. Helena Basket. I'm going to hell in a basket. You've got to humor me because I'm going crazy. Everything's hazy and I'm daft as a daisy. You understand, don't you?"

Roz didn't, of course. But she did lie down, and when Pidge's body rested upon hers and Pidge's lips found hers, Roz gave up understanding. And why not, she wondered. If you were an animal you didn't draw lines. If you were an animal you might as well be an animal all the way, and if you could make another animal happy in the process, well, why on earth hold back?

Besides, Pidge's mouth was soft and Pidge's hands were hungry. And Roz wanted it now, wanted it very much, wanted it and didn't care at all whether a man or a woman was the one giving her what she wanted. It didn't matter. When you were an animal nothing mattered, nothing at all.

You just lay there, and you let your whole body throb with the feelings that were coursing through you, and the world spun like a top, and the sky turned inside-out and upside down and moved in on her like wolves on lambs, and the earth opened up and it rained for forty days and forty nights, and she was in the ark with the other animals, safe and sound, snug as a bug in a rug, her whole body vibrating and spinning and reeling in a response that was terrifying in its intensity.

It got better and better, with Pidge everywhere and doing everything, and the room rocking and rolling like an adolescent entertainer, and better and better and better and higher and higher.

And it ended well. Not a sharp climax like a thunderclap but a gentle reaching and groping until suddenly the tension began to dissipate, the passion rolled away, the tensions drained and left her, Roz Robshaw, lying on her back in a feverish room with a cool head and empty eyes, holding in her arms a warm frightened girl who whimpered like a wet puppy and talked and talked and talked without making any sense at all, talking and talking, rhyming words and making up new words, her mouth spilling out all the confusion in her poor twisted head.

LINDA PIERCE HAD A short fuse to begin with. The pre-party festivities with Walt Forsythe, who had been so decidedly uncooperative, and with Steve Gordon, who had managed to get her hot without helping to cool her off, had only succeeded in shortening that fuse to the point where it no longer existed.

She was a bomb dying to go off.

But she couldn't go off, not without a man. And there was no man around to help her out. She had to sit by herself and watch a pair of dykes doing things to each other and, by the way, to her own blood pressure, waiting for her turn in the limelight.

God!

It was bad, sitting and watching Peggy and Mary. Her own inclinations didn't run to that sort of thing, although there had been one drunken evening at Clifton College so many years ago when her roommate, a pretty brunette named Ruth Hardy, had initiated her into the pleasantries of lesbian behavior. It had been nice, but it had not been her cup of tea. Little Linda Pierce, whose maiden name had been Shepard, was interested strictly in men.

But where the hell were the men?

She couldn't wait much longer. Finally Peggy and Mary got finished and wandered off-stage, Mary glowing, Peggy looking all drawn and hollow-eyed, and the stage was empty. For a moment Linda waited patiently for Walt Forsythe to step to the stage and announce the next act. But her patience was not the enduring sort, and when Walt failed to appear at once she decided that she simply could not wait any longer. She knew what the next act was going to be. *She* was going to be the next act, and if they didn't like it they could go and lump it.

An excellent idea.

Stirring.

Striking.

Satisfying.

A simple act. Just Linda Pierce and men, and the more the merrier, and if the audience didn't get their kicks out of that sort of stuff, well, it was just too goddamned bad.

Let them go off in a corner and shoot themselves, if they wanted.

She got up and walked to the stage. She carried herself perfectly, her blonde hair flowing over her creamy shoulders, her breasts jutting out like rampant melons, her buttocks sashaying gently from side to side as she walked. She was a symphony of sex and she knew it.

She mounted the stage and stood in the spotlight. It made her body even more attractive, which was saying one hell of a lot. Her voice had a rasp to it and she practically spat out her words.

"The next act," she said, her eyes flashing, "consists of me. Since it is not a solo number because I outgrew that sort of thing in early adolescence, I shall require some assistance. I want the following men to come to the stage: Steve Gordon, Bill Jansen, Joe Robshaw and Walt Forsythe. Hurry, gentlemen!"

Linda waited while the men walked to the stage to join her. Her heart was pounding and she was too excited to stand still. She kept shifting her weight from one foot to the other and back again, her body warm and feverish, her palms damp with her own perspiration, her eyes hot and her mouth dry.

She watched the men. Bill Jansen was first in line and Linda smiled when she saw him, remembering the other time they had been together. But Bill had changed since then. He had a childish look in his eyes and she thought to herself that Bill was as batty as his wife. They made a charming couple.

Well, she'd give him his money's worth.

Next Joe Robshaw, his eyes turned to the floor, walking slouched over and seemingly uninterested in what was going on. She'd liven the bastard up, damn him. She'd show him what it was all about.

Then Steve Gordon, looking like the Noble Savage, all ready and willing for action. And after him Walter Forsythe, amused and involved all at once, the old master at the game of love.

They'd get theirs. And she would get hers. Everybody would have themselves a ball.

"You first, Bill," she told him. "The rest of you can stand around and watch."

She took Bill and led him to the bed. He told her not to worry, that he would put on a good show for the people and that everybody would enjoy it, and she kissed him and touched him and rubbed her own tense warmness against him, and then he stopped talking and began performing. He performed very well. She thought, when it was all over, that he ought to receive an Oscar for his performance, or, at the very least, a Beauregard.

But she didn't have time to mull this over. It was an intriguing line of thought, but there was a time for thought and a time for action, and she tended to think that the present happened to be the time for action.

So she dismissed Bill Jansen simultaneously from her body and from her mind, waved him away with one hand and beckoned to Joe Robshaw with the other.

"Next!"

And Joe went to her. He went to her automatically, coldly, and it took a little hard work on her part to get him interested enough to do what she wanted him to do to her. His heart was not in it, not at all, but something else was, and that was all she cared about.

It began, it endured, it ended.

"Next!"

Chapter 14

IN THE ENTIRE ROOM, only two persons managed to watch everything that went on without feeling the slightest iota of excitement. They watched Peggy and Mary, watched Linda first with Bill and then with Joe and then with Steve and finally with Walt. They watched every detail without feeling anything at all.

It did not move them.

But they watched, and they remained calm. They were waiting their turn. Soon it would be their chance to take their place in the sun and go through the paces of their own particular act.

Soon.

And then Walt Forsythe was standing on the stage, looking more than a little worn down from his turn with Linda, and he was looking out at the audience with a peculiar smile on his face.

"Next," he was saying, "we have another rather pleasant sort of diversion for you in the persons of Mark Phillips and Sue Carson. I'm sure everyone will find their demonstration quite entertaining, if a bit bizarre. Let's give them a great big hand!"

Nobody applauded.

"Places, please!"

Quickly, precisely, Mark and Sue walked to the stage. She was naked. He was almost naked, but not quite. He was wearing a belt around his waist, a black alligator belt, which looked slightly ridiculous in view of the fact that he was not wearing any pants.

Just a belt.

The belt looked quite purposeless. But, as it turned out, the belt had a purpose.

A definite purpose.

Sue crouched on the bed, her breasts downward, her head lowered. Her back was to the audience, with her buttocks thrust at them like an offering to a god.

An appealing offering.

Mark approached her. He passed a hand over her buttocks, the gesture tender and loving. Then he drew back his hand and slapped her, making a mockery of the tender gesture, and when he drew his hand away there was a red mark where he had struck her.

Then he removed the belt.

He took his time, swinging the belt loosely in his hand, taking careful aim. Then the belt whistled through the air and struck.

Sue screamed.

There was a collective gasp from the audience.

Before the gasp ended the belt was swinging through

the air once more, landing with a harsh sickening sound against the girl's soft rump.

Another scream.

It was only the beginning.

BILL JANSEN FOUND NANCY Gordon in the darkness. It wasn't easy, but he searched around until he found her, crawling from mattress to mattress on his hands and knees in much the same manner that his wife had crawled to Roz Robshaw.

He had to look carefully to find Nancy Gordon, but that didn't matter. It was an important thing for him to find her and Bill Jansen was not the sort to attempt to shirk his responsibilities. When there was something that he had to do, well, by George, he did it. You had to play the game, had to do what you were supposed to do, or people would be disappointed.

And it wouldn't do to disappoint people, not when they were counting on you.

So long. So many long years of people counting on you and you had to work hard and be careful not to disappoint them. His mother first, and his father, pushing him to work hard and get the highest marks in school, pushing him so that he could be very good and very important and they could be proud of him. All the things he had wanted to do, but couldn't do, because they were counting on him to become an important man and he didn't want them to be disappointed.

And now everybody was counting on him. He had to put on a good show for everybody, for all the people watching the movie, and he had to do it with Nancy Gordon. Because poor Nancy Gordon was all alone. And that wouldn't do at all—she had to participate. Everybody had to participate or they would be shirking their responsibilities.

He found her, finally. And he put his lips to her ear and told her very earnestly that she had to play the game or she would be shirking her job.

She seemed amused. She looked at him as though he was a little boy and smiled.

"I'm sorry," she said. "I'm afraid I'm not in condition just now."

He didn't understand.

"Come on," he said. He reached clumsily for her breast, his fingers closing around her nipple. She tried to pull away but the sexual stimulation of the evening thus far was a little too much for her. The nipple went rigid and she drew in her breath very sharply, feeling her body begin to respond in spite of herself.

She heaved a sigh, pulling free of him. "Look," she said, "I'm not in condition. You're a married man. You ought to know about these things."

He looked puzzled.

"Once a month," she explained, painfully, "a certain type of activity becomes impossible. Now do you understand, for God's sake?"

"Oh," he said. "Your period."

"Yes, my period. My monthlies, my curse, whatever the hell you want to call it. No matter how you look at it I'm out of circulation, and if I'd known it was going to start I wouldn't have come to the damned meeting tonight, and if you don't get your damned hands off my damned breasts I am going to go out of my mind."

"Your period," he said.

"Yes, stupid. My—"

"There are other ways," he cut in.

"Maybe I don't like them."

"But you have to. I mean, everybody'll be so disappointed otherwise. You don't want to disappoint them, do you?"

He touched her breasts again and she knew that she was going to have to give in to him or go stark raving mad. Her breasts felt as though they were burning up and his hands were not helping matters any.

"Tell me about it," she said.

He told her.

"I'm sorry," she said. "That particular method doesn't appeal to me."

"It doesn't?"

"No. It's dirty."

"Please, Nancy—"

"I'm sorry," she said, wondering to herself why she had such a feeling of repugnance for what he had suggested. "I'm sorry, but my lips are sealed."

He grinned ingratiatingly. "You know," he told her, his hands still at work on her breasts, "there are certain other ways."

Now it was her turn to look puzzled.

"Look at it this way," he suggested. "The main entrance is out of order and the window won't open. What do we do, now?"

She didn't know.

"We use the back door," he told her. "Roll over, will you?"

"THE TROUBLE WITH YOU," Steve Gordon told Peggy Phillips, "is that you don't know what it's like with a real man."

"I know what it's like."

"Not with me," he insisted. "Just with that little squirt you got for a husband. You don't know what it's like with me."

"Honey," she cooed. "Honey, I tried it with you. Don't you remember?"

He remembered.

"And I didn't like it."

"You will," he said. "We're going to try it again, and to-night you are going to like it. You're going to like it so much you're going to go out of your mind."

She sighed. She just wanted him to go away. He was a man, another man, and she didn't want to see another man as long as she lived. Men were like Mark, sadistic pigs who only wanted to ruin a woman.

"It's unnatural," Steve was telling her. "You doing it with a woman. It's disgusting."

He reached for her. She started to pull away, then changed her mind. After all, she told herself, what earthly difference did it make? Let him have his hoggish fun, let him get it over with so he would leave her alone. That was all she wanted, just to be left alone until it was time for her to go away.

"All right," she said.

It began, and she even went through the movements, determined to do such a good job at it that he would be properly impressed. She did a good job, acting like a machine, lying there and moving with him and feeling nothing at all, nothing, but physical movement that couldn't have meant less to her if it had been happening to somebody else in another room with the door shut. It was a temporary violation of her body, but she took her mind out, far out into space, and told herself that nothing at all was happening, that it was just a dream from which she would awake in time.

It ended, and he raised himself from her, and he looked at her, his face one huge ridiculous smile of self-satisfaction.

And he asked her how it was.

And she told him, her own heart smiling as she watched his face fall apart.

IT WAS A SPECTACULAR party. The party seemed to be predicated on the premise that twelve people could have just as much fun as sixteen people, and the twelve people there certainly seemed to be having more fun than the sixteen who had been gathered in the same room just a week ago. The party went on, gathering momentum as it went, and when it finally ended and the final guest left, Walt Forsythe looked at his wife and smiled.

Things were going well. Things were going very well, and there was no telling just where it would all lead. It could be fun, and that, in the final analysis, was all that seemed to matter.

Walt and Mary cleaned up the room, then went downstairs to put the living room into a semblance of order. The job downstairs turned out to be an easy one—the house surely did not look as though it had been the scene of that type of party.

But it had.

No scars on the house, Walt thought. No scars at all. The party had been held, and the end result as far as the house itself was concerned was far more mild than at a good many more, moderate parties.

The only scars were on the guests themselves.

Chapter 15

THE PARTY AT WHICH movies had been shown knocked four members from the roster of sixteen. The next party, which featured live theatre, accounted for the loss of three more. Whether it was the party itself which was responsible or whether the dropping of these three members was part of the normal course of events is in the nature of a moot point. Either way, Roz and Joe Robshaw as well as Peggy Phillips were not on hand for the next meeting.

As you may have noted, this chronicle of events has taken a definite established pattern. The parties themselves serve as points of crystallization, as it were. Each party is responsible for various changes in the characters of various individuals. A percentage of these individuals in turn drop from the circle and are dismissed, no longer deserving consideration.

But first, of course, we must study the manner in which the drop occurs. With the Robshaws, first, and then with Peggy Phillips.

If Joe and Roz Robshaw arrived at the party in a state somewhat reminiscent of a Yogic trance, they left it in a state of pure emotional decay. They did not talk on the way home because they had absolutely nothing to say to each other. Roz was wearing the tight sweater and tighter skirt that she had arrived in and she looked more sluttish than ever. Her makeup was smeared all over her pretty face. There were deep circles under her eyes and she smelled of sex.

Joe, who had arrived looking like an unmade bed, now looked like an unmade bed that had been the scene of whirlwind sexual activity. His suit was a mess, his face was a mess, and he relaxed behind the steering wheel in a position which suggested that he had been born without a backbone.

They rode in silence. He put the car in the garage and they went inside, undressing and tumbling into bed without even bothering to wash themselves or brush their teeth. They both had a good deal of trouble getting to sleep, but they lay on opposite sides of their bed without talking, without seeming to notice that they were together.

Finally they slept—not well—and when morning came they wished it would go away. But it didn't, and they got up and showered and ate what might have been called a leisurely breakfast except for the fact that the phrase suggests a feeling of well-being and contentment which hardly existed for them.

Sunday passed, and Monday. Joe called in sick to the office on Monday, the first time he had done so in years. He generally went to work no matter how vile he felt, occasionally trekking down to Wall Street while running a fever. This time there was nothing physically wrong with Joe whatsoever. He simply did not feel like going to work, so he called in and told them he was sick. They were sympathetic, told him to take things easy, he was a valuable man, he'd been working himself too hard, he should come in whenever be felt like it and not worry about a thing.

As he put the phone back on the hook he thought for a moment that he was not exactly playing fair with them, that he was taking advantage of his business relationship and cheating his employers. He knew that he ought to feel guilty about it, but somehow the guilt feelings failed to come. He shrugged, found the morning paper, read the comics and the sports pages and spent the day lounging around the house doing nothing.

Roz joined him in that she didn't do anything either. She let the dishes stay in the sink, let the beds remain un-made, and took a private little vacation all her own. Again they did not talk, mainly because neither had anything to say to the other.

And Monday passed.

Tuesday Joe still didn't feel like going to work. He called in, told them he was still feeling rotten, agreed with them that he ought to see a doctor, and told them it would be good to get back in the saddle as soon as possible. Then he spent the rest of the morning with the comics and the sports page, and his pipe. He didn't even bother getting dressed. He just lay around the house in his pajamas.

Breakfast that morning was frozen orange juice, dry cereal and instant coffee. Roz just couldn't be bothered with cooking anything. It also looked as though they were going to run into problems in the near future, because they were rapidly running out of clean dishes and she would be damned if she was going to take the trouble to wash one.

They missed lunch.

Things came to a head somewhere around the middle of the afternoon. The situation was an artificial one and both of them must have recognized the fact. It could only go on so long, and it went on as long as it could. The air was ready to be cleared; all that remained was for one of them to make the first move.

Roz made it. She walked into the living room, pulled a chair over to where Joe was sitting and sat in it. For a little while he ignored her, but finally he looked up at her.

"I can't take any more of this," she told him. "I'll go out of my mind."

He nodded.

"We've got to do something."

"A divorce?"

"I suppose I've been thinking of that. Is that what you want?"

"I'm not sure."

"If it is," she said, "we can work something out. Or if you'd prefer a trial separation, we could try something along those lines. All I know is that things can't go on the way they've been going. Those parties—"

"I know."

"Do you know what I did Saturday? Do you know that I made love with a woman simply because I didn't have anything better to do?"

He hung his head. "I was no model of decorum myself. You must have seen me with Linda Pierce."

She nodded.

"It's no good, Roz. I don't enjoy it. Neither do you. We're just letting ourselves go without knowing what we're doing or why we're doing it."

"I know, Joe."

"Maybe it's all right for some people. The Forsythes— nothing seems to touch them. Or some of the others. But we're not built for that kind of stuff. It was a kick at first, I'll admit that much. Now it's not even a kick any longer. It's as if we're trying to see just how far we can go before we can't even stomach ourselves any more."

"It's worse than that," she said. "It's . . . it's sick, terribly sick. I don't understand myself. I thought I was a good woman—"

He didn't say anything.

"I thought we were a good couple. I know we didn't have much in common, we weren't a pair of faceless parts out of the pages of *McCall's*, but I didn't think that had anything to do with it. I loved you and you loved me and I thought that was going to be enough. But then everything went all out of proportion. What the hell happened to us,

Joe? What happened to us? Why did we come apart? I don't understand it."

"Neither do I."

"You did love me, didn't you?"

He took a long look at her, his mouth half-open, and then he said the only right thing, which also happened to be the only thing he could say.

He said: "I still do."

And she looked at him for a moment, a long moment, and listened to what he had said, and saw things much more clearly all at once, and opened her mouth because there was something she had to say now, and closed her mouth again because the words wouldn't come, and then all at once broke up completely.

The tears came slowly at first. Then the floodgates came all the way open and tears streamed down her face. She was a big woman and she cried like a big woman, her shoulders heaving, her chest wrenched with sobs, her tears all salty and bitter. Joe did the right thing again, moving to her, holding her, patting her back, not saying a word because there was nothing to be said just then.

And, all at once, she knew that she had to stay with this man, this strong man who loved her and who was the only man she had ever loved. And, at the same time, he knew that this was the only woman for him, that he needed her with him forever, that without her he was nothing and would always be nothing, that with her he still had a chance to survive.

The pact was sealed in silence.

It was that simple, and yet it wasn't that simple. She still had a lot of crying to do because there were a lot of tears and a lot of bad things built up within her that should have come out long ago. And they both had a lot of thinking to do, the silent thinking which two people become capable of when they know each other well and when they are able to share a mood.

Then they sat and talked, and told each other that they were going to begin anew, that it was going to be all right, that everything would be all right. And Joe called the office again, told them he wanted two weeks for a vacation, knowing that they would probably say no and that if they did he would quit his job and look for another one later.

But they did not say no, they told him they knew something had been bothering him and he should stay out as long as he had to until everything was straightened out. And he put down the phone with relief, and he went to her, and then he called the airport for reservations and told her to get to work packing a pair of suitcases.

Which she did.

So they flew to Florida, took a little cottage on the Gulf Coast near Sarasota, spent their days lying in the sun and swimming in the water, spent their nights in each other's arms.

And it worked.

The wounds were deep and the wounds took time healing, but eventually the wounds did heal and they were one again. They were close now, very close, and the little things that kept them apart were suddenly quite inconsequential in comparison to the big things that kept them together. They were in love, and they needed each other, and they were lost without each other, and that and nothing else was what really mattered to them.

They came back from Florida, suntanned and healthy, and Joe went back to his job and Roz went back to her house, and they went to work.

There were still hard times. There was the memory of the sickness, the memory of the arms and mouths and bodies of other men and other women, and these memories were bad ones. But time fades memories and in time the memories faded.

They found new friends, and they found a new way of life, and life was good to them.

They adopted a child.

They turned into a family.

They liked being a family. It was nice, being not two people named Joe and Roz but being an entity, The Robshaws, with a little boy to prove it.

And, perhaps because of the change in them, they had a child of their own. This happens, sometimes, when a couple adopts a child. The one of their own was a girl, and the two kids together did quite a lot for them. They were good kids. And Joe and Roz were good parents.

So we can bid a fond adieu to the Robshaws. As the storybooks say, they lived happily ever after. Let's forget them, huh?

WHEN PEGGY PHILLIPS FINALLY got up the nerve to leave it was a cold rainy Friday morning. The kids, God bless them, were in school. Mark, God bless him, was at work. There was nothing for Peggy to stay home with, and consequently no reason for Peggy to stay home.

So she didn't.

She packed a suitcase, wondering at first how she would fit everything she needed into a single suitcase, then discovering that she really didn't have that much to take along after all.

Just some clothes. Just an extra pair of shoes and a few extra pairs of stockings and a dress and a skirt and a sweater. She didn't want to take too many clothes because the girl she finally met might want her to dress in some particular way, and if that were the case she would only have to throw her own clothes away anyway, so there was little point in taking them.

And there was one thing she wouldn't need any longer. She would not need her diaphragm. That was one thing she could sure as hell get along without.

That was another thing—you didn't have to worry when you did it with a woman. There was no lousy little brat to come along and spoil your life for you, no kid to get in the way all the time. Just love, pure love, with no annoying little dividends that kept needing their diapers changed.

She laughed. Then abruptly she stopped laughing, picked up her suitcase and left the house. She locked the door, but she hadn't bothered to take her key with her. She wasn't going to need it. She was never coming back there again.

At the station, when she asked for a ticket to New York, the ticket-seller asked her whether she wanted a one-way ticket or a round-trip ticket.

"One way," she told him. "I am never coming back here."

He looked at her oddly for a second or two, a bit taken aback at the tone of her voice, and then gave her her ticket and her change. She waited for the train, boarded it, gave her ticket to the conductor and sat back patiently while the train found its way to Grand Central Station.

For a moment, after she was off the train and all alone in the middle of Grand Central Station with only a suitcase for company, she hadn't the slightest idea where to go. Then she decided that the right place was Greenwich Village, that all the girls like her were supposed to live there, so she dragged her suitcase to the nearest taxi and told the cab driver to take her to Greenwich Village.

"Big place," he told her. "Any particular part of the Village you want to go to? Any kind of an address you can give me?"

She thought of telling him to take her to a lesbian hangout, *any* lesbian hangout, and then laughed at the thought of how he would probably react. It would be funny, but she didn't have time to play games.

"An inexpensive hotel," she told him. "Not a rat-trap, but nothing too expensive."

The driver knew a place and drove her there. It was on West Fourth Street near Washington Square and the rent was only twenty dollars a week. It would do, she decided, until she either found a good apartment of her own or a girl to live with.

She spent the rest of the day and the two days that followed simply wandering around the Village, getting used to the feel of the place. She liked it—for the first time in her life she had found a location in which she was instantly and completely at home. The informal atmosphere, the little shops, the odd people, the strange small buildings right in the heart of New York—all these things were very appealing to her.

But the best part was still to come.

On the fourth night in New York she found the place she had been searching for without knowing it from the moment she left Eastport. It was a bar, not noticeably different on the outside from any of a few dozen other Village bars she had passed in her wanderings. But on the inside it was very different.

All the customers were women.

Some of them were so masculine in appearance that

they might have passed for men in other surroundings. Those, Peggy knew, were the butches, and she had no particular desire to meet one of them. They were like men, and she was not interested in men. Men were like Steve and Mark and Walt and all the others. If she wanted a man she could have a real man, not these silly boy-girls.

The other women were more interesting. On the surface they looked no more "queer" than Peggy did. But inside they were like her, lesbians, girls who found their love with other girls. When Peggy walked into the bar she could feel them looking at her, sizing her up, and it made her feel all warm inside.

She went to the bar, bought a drink and took it to a table. It wasn't long before somebody joined her, a long-limbed redhead named Terri James.

They had two more drinks apiece, and then Peggy went home with Terri James to a well-furnished little apartment on Bedford Street in the West Village. It was a nice apartment, and Terri was a wonderful lover, and things proceeded very slowly and very magically and very delightfully.

First Terri put a few records on the hi-fi, good Italian baroque chamber music scored for harpsichord, flute, bassoon, and oboe. The music was very clean and very precise, the counterpoint interesting, the melodies imaginative. It was light airy music, and listening to it was like taking a soothing bath.

Then they talked and they got to know each other, and

that in itself was good. Men didn't want to get to know you. All they were interested in was sex, the act itself, and the preliminaries, the sharing of ideas and emotions, were out of their reach.

Not so with Terri.

And then, when they knew each other, it began very slowly and very well. Terri came to her, and took her face between her two clean hands, and kissed her on the mouth. It was a sisterly sort of kiss and Peggy liked it. No one had done that to her before, not since Andy, and Andy was something that happened long ago and far away.

The next kiss was not sisterly at all. It was passionate, and the passion grabbed Peggy up and whirled her around, and she wanted to do things but Terri told her just to relax, that she would do everything.

So Peggy relaxed, lying there passive on Terri's bed while Terri undressed her and made love to her. It was so very different from what had happened with Mary, so much cleaner and fresher and more alive, and it was so unbelievably good she couldn't be sure it was real.

It was. And it got better and better and she was so completely caught up in it that she began to make little animal sounds in her throat without knowing that she was making any sounds at all. Her whole body writhed and twisted under Terri's skilled touch, Terri's kisses on her breasts and Terri's tender hands on her hot moist thighs, Terri's passionate tongue coursing over her smooth golden stomach and working its way down, driving her into a frenzy and pitching her passion to the boiling point.

It was hot, so hot she was burning up, and cold, so cold she was freezing. It was hot and cold, up and down, back and forth, wet and dry, black and white, good and evil. It was beyond good and evil, bigger than life, larger than life, better than life.

More. More. More . . .

And the world whistled, and the moon turned to black, and the music dipped and soared, and it went on.

And on. And on.

Until it was too good to be true, and the crest was reached and passed, and her heart sang and sang like a hopped-up robin, and the sky fell in very gently and bathed her in the soft warm glow of love.

And she slept, her arms around Terri's good body, her cheek on Terry's full breast.

It would no doubt be pleasant to report that Peggy and Terri lived happily ever after. This, however, did not happen to be the way things worked out. They lived happily for approximately three weeks, snug as two bugs in a rug in the cozy little apartment on Grove Street. Then they broke up, and Peggy cried, and after awhile she went back to the lesbian bar and found another girl and went home with her.

There was a regular parade from then on. Sometimes the alliances lasted as long as a year, sometimes no more than a single passionate night. Sometimes it was the new girl who moved in with Peggy rather than the other way around.

But always there was a contentment, even with all the unrest, even with the inevitable periodic disruptions of her life. Each new affair seemed likely at the onset to go on forever, and as each old affair disintegrated the hurts became less and less and the joys became more and more.

Sometimes she thought about her children, but not often. Because, at the bottom of it all, she did not love her children any more than she loved Mark. She loved only herself, and for this reason she could only love other women, people like herself.

She found an apartment of her own, found a job clerking in a Village jewelry shop, and the time passed. She had her life, and while there might well have been better lives, this was the only one she could be happy with. It was hers, fitting her as well as her own skin, and she lived with it and liked it.

THOSE THREE, THEN, MAY be forgotten. Joe and Roz and Peggy, gone their separate ways into separate lives. We may forget them. We still have the group to consider.

Nine of them.

Steve and Nancy Gordon.

Walt and Mary Forsythe.

Sue Carson and Mark Phillips—since Sue moved in with Mark the minute Peggy disappeared, moved in and took care of the children.

Bill and Pidge Jansen.

And Linda Pierce.

They lived through the week in their own separate ways, lived through it and lived for Saturday night. There was no question but that they would all be present at the party. That went without saying.

In the meanwhile Linda Pierce played the role of the nymphomaniac, Sue Carson and Mark Phillips settled down to a man-and-wife relationship marred only by their personal deviations, and the rest played out their own parts as man and wife.

And waited for Saturday.

Saturday was bright, the sun shining, the lawns green, the air crisp and clear.

Saturday faded, the sun setting, the air cooling off, the sky darkening.

Evening came, and with it the party.

Chapter 16

THE PARTY WAS A party.

A full description of what went on at Walt and Mary Forsythe's that Saturday night is hardly necessary and would hardly be interesting even if it were. It was a party not unlike the other two parties, a party with nine present instead of twelve or sixteen, and at this particular party it became obvious to just about everybody that the group didn't have much of a future.

This much should have been obvious. There was a desperate quality to the sex itself, as if the participants were working to generate enthusiasm for a novelty which had outlived its novel stage and had become a routine. Events followed what had by now become their normal course, and people leaped from one body to the next with little feeling and little desire.

When the party ended, no one was especially sorry that it was over. It ended with a surge of relief, as if those present were tremendously pleased with themselves with having lived through another one. They went their separate ways, unmoved and immobile, unshocked and unshockable, unexcited and quite unexcitable.

They did not know it, not for a fact, but that was the last party the club ever held.

Whether there could have been another meeting of the group if the course of events during the next week had been different is a difficult question to answer satisfactorily, a moot point at best. Suffice it to say that the same factors which led to the spiritual dissolution of the group were finally responsible for certain more concrete reasons for the total dispersal of the organization. It had become inevitable.

A favored historical explanation for the fall of the Roman empire, leaning away from earlier single-cause theories which blamed anything from poor soil to the spread of Christianity for the fall of Rome, suggests that the fall was a consequence of the rise. In other words, the rising of Rome had been such as to develop such a state that the consequent decline and fall became inevitable.

The same line of reasoning might well be applied to our little Roman Empire in microcosm. The nature of the group, the manner of its formation, the very reason for its existence, was such that it could not endure for any great length of time. It had to dissolve itself, just as Rome had to fall, just as for every action there is an equal and opposite reaction. Physical laws are astounding constants—they apply to suburban social groups just as surely as to city-states and atomic dust.

We have watched the club, studied the members, seen the club form itself and then begin to go. All that remains is what might be called, to continue our analogy, the sack of Rome by the legions of Attila. Barbarian invasions are always fun when watched from the sidelines—Hollywood knows this, and Hollywood develops its own armies of Goths and Huns and Vandals and turns out vile pictures by the carload. Some day these barbaric hordes may well overrun Hollywood, a pleasant prospect. But that is neither here nor there.

Remember, we have our circle of nine still to be considered. Walt and Mary Forsythe, Sue Carson and Mark Phillips, Bill and Pidge Jansen, Steve and Nancy Gordon, and Linda Pierce. Their lives are still part of our study, and we must study them.

Watch closely.

PERHAPS THE MOST SIGNIFICANT event of the party, a sin of omission for a change rather than a sin of commission, was the utter impotence of Bill Jansen. We might even make a play on words and call it a sin of omission as opposed to a sin of emission. At any rate, the facts are plain and simple. Bill Jansen found himself quite incapable of acquitting himself nobly on the field of battle. The spirit was willing but the flesh was lamentably weak.

He tried. No one ever tried harder, or more valiantly, and no one took failure quite so stoically. At least it appeared that way. The spirit was willing at first, and then more willing, and finally downright insistent. But the flesh remained persistently weak, and the desired result was not achieved.

Most men might have accepted the failure for what it was—a temporary thing, and certainly no cause for worry. Bill Jansen might have done the same thing—a year ago, or a month ago, or a week ago. Now, however, it was just too much.

He had failed. That was all he could think about, in the room at the party, in the car on the way home, in the bedroom that he shared with Pidge. He had failed miserably and now everybody would be disappointed in him. He was supposed to put on a good show, and what had he done? Nothing, nothing at all.

He was an orator tongue-tied, a dancer crippled, a musician gone tone-deaf. He had failed, failed completely, and that was all there was to it.

And Pidge, of course, was no help at all. She seemed to find the episode somewhat hysterical, and she was laughing her pretty head off. This in itself might have been indicative of very little, since Pidge laughed all the time lately, laughed shrilly and hysterically, made up funny rhymes and went off into peals of laughter at her own esoteric humor.

But now her laughter was all he needed. Just what the doctor ordered, for God's sake. It wasn't bad enough being a failure—he had to have his wife keep reminding him of the fact.

And off she went, laughing that shrill and evil laugh,

laughing like a madwoman, her voice cracking at the high point of her laughter and her eyes rolling about like marbles in a child's game.

It was terrible.

Failure.

The one word kept ringing in his head that and *disappointment*. He was a disappointment to his wife, a disappointment to the audience, a disappointment to everybody around him.

To his parents, who had been counting on him to make good, who now had their trust betrayed. What would his mother think of him if she saw him now? What would his father think?

Failure.

Disappointment.

Disappointing failure.

Failing disappointment.

Over and over, the same words banging against the inside of his head until he was sick to his stomach, running to the bathroom and barely making it in time, emptying his stomach of its contents, throwing up over and over again until nothing more came out and he merely gagged nauseously again and again.

Failure.

Disappointment.

Failure and disappointment.

He left the bathroom finally, determined to win this

time, determined to satisfy the audience that had always demanded too much of him, determined to get it done with once and for all, to erase the blot of failure and make his record perfect once again. He went to Pidge, to the mad little girl in their mad little bed, and lay down beside her and reached for her.

She rolled her eyes and stuck out her tongue and her laughter cut the room in half.

And her words—wild rhyming words with a logic all their own, words that he didn't understand but that hurt just the same.

"No balls for curtain calls, flirtin' with the curtain and running up the halls, catcalls, bat calls, round calls and flat calls—"

And more laughter.

And the failure that he dreaded came to him and took him in its arms. He touched Pidge and his hands raced up and down her body but there was no response, no response at all.

Failure.

Disappointment.

Failure and disappointment.

He ran from the bedroom, ran to the bathroom to be sick again, then sat down in the bathroom and locked the door to keep the world away. Long ago he had locked the bathroom door, long ago when he was a child and a locked bathroom meant security for the practice of secret guilt. And he locked it now.

And sat alone.

With failure.

And in one hand he took that part of himself that had failed, that part that would not perform, that disappointed everybody, and he held it in his hand.

In the other hand he held a razor blade.

And, because he could not live with that sort of failure, and because he was mad at that part of himself, which was destroying his life, he did what seemed the only thing to do.

He bled to death with his failure clutched tight in a death-grip.

PIDGE CALLED THE POLICE, somehow and when they broke down the door and found him, it was the end for her just as it had been the end for him. The police looked at her and listened to her and sent in a rush call, and the men came and put Pidge in a straitjacket and led her away to a place where it was cool and quiet.

Where she remained.

They gave her shock treatments, which did not help, and they gave her group therapy sessions, which did not help, and they worked constantly with her, and this did not help either.

And, finally, they left her alone. This was no great help either, but it was the best thing possible. She was not un-happy—she was quite contented, with a pleasant room to live in and books to read and her own thoughts spinning through her mind. She was quiet, except when some of her own private thoughts were very funny indeed and she sailed off into wild and uncontrollable peals of laughter. This happened often at first, but as time passed she grew more and more silent, sitting still most of the time and living her own life in her own unfortunate mind.

IF BILL JANSEN CRACKED up and his wife fell apart, Steve and Nancy Gordon simply dissolved. They had been the untouchable ones in the group, their nerves never tightening up on them, their appetites never wandering too far from the ordinary.

The only thing was that they found it quite useless to go on living together.

It took a few days from the time of the final party. Then they began to realize that they had married without being in love and that they had not grown in love. They were living together as man and wife, but their mutual inadequacy made them look to sex orgies for their own entertainment.

This, they were beginning to realize, was not essentially healthy.

It did not happen overnight. It took the better part of a week of calm discussion and rather deep introspection, but before the week was out they agreed that they were not in love, that there was relatively little chance of their ever falling in love, and marriage had become something of a farce.

So they decided to end it.

It was all done quietly, reasonably, sensibly. Nancy took a plane to Las Vegas to establish residency for a quick Nevada divorce. Steve listed the house with a real estate agent, not needing such a large place by himself and moved to a Manhattan apartment. The divorce went through and they were single again.

Both of them eventually remarried. Nancy remarried several times, each time failing to find the love she was looking for, each time returning to Nevada and getting started all over again.

Steve tried one more time, missed, and remained a bachelor after that. He took up bachelor quarters in the East Sixties, devoting much of his time to his favorite hobby, the pursuit of willing female flesh. He was quite successful and he enjoyed himself tremendously.

Perhaps the Gordon marriage was doomed from the start—they married in the first place without knowing or loving each other, and both love and knowledge are rather necessary for a good marriage.

Yet it is altogether possible that they would have grown to love one another, that a relationship that began as a mistake might have turned into a worthwhile thing. This happens often enough. Many people marry by mistake, as it were, recognize their mistake, make the most of it, and wonder years later how they could have thought of it as a mistake. Love is a slow and mysterious animal, as likely to develop after marriage as before.

But they did not have the chance. Not in Eastport, not in the charming circle of friends led by Walt Forsythe. There they grew too fast, and grew apart, and their marriage was over before it had really begun.

In a sense they were quite fortunate. They did not die, or go mad, or become twisted little people in the grip of perversion. They were divorced, a not uncommon occurrence in twentieth century America.

Just divorced.

Worse things could have happened.

Chapter 17

IF THE END CAME for Steve and Nancy with their divorce, the end for Mark Phillips and Sue Carson consisted of their living together forever. They remained together in Mark's house with Mark's children, not married legally until several changes occurred—a decree for Sue on grounds of desertion, a decree for Mark on similar grounds. Their mates had left them and they were together.

Sue was a quiet person who became quieter with the passage of time. Mark was a mean man who became steadily more cruel to her.

In a very real sense they were stuck with each other, stuck with themselves and their own warped desires. They could not separate because each of them fulfilled a very genuine need of the other. They were inextricably united, joined for life.

They were not happy. Happiness was one thing which was always denied to them. They were not the sort of people with a chance for anything resembling happiness. They were what they were. There was virtually nothing to be done about it.

Sue craved punishment. This craving stemmed from a

variety of reasons, none of them too important in the final analysis. She needed to be dominated, and to be subdued, and to be humiliated, and to be tormented, and to be hurt.

She got what she needed.

Mark needed to punish, to hurt, to be cruel and domineering and unkind. This craving also stemmed from any number of innate personality defects, and again the specific causes are quite irrelevant in the end. He needed to punish and to hurt and to be cruel and domineering and unkind.

And he got what he needed.

The physical aspect of their relationship gradually diminished in its intensity. Words can hurt more than whips and tongues can cut more deeply than knives. Mental cruelty is far more effective than physical cruelty, and a tormented mind screams louder and more insistently than tormented flesh.

He inflicted pain and she received it. And they lived together because they could not live apart, taking their pleasure in their pain, living twisted lives in a twisted world.

LINDA PIERCE, THE BLONDE bombshell with the yen for men, went on along established lines. There were no tremendous changes in her basic make-up, except for the fact that she eventually ran out of money.

At which time she did the perfectly logical thing for a woman in her particular set of circumstances. She put her hobby on a paying basis and turned it into a profession.

She had the body for it, and the face for it, and she definitely had the inclinations for it. She wanted men, and men were precisely what she got. She set out to be the best damned whore in the United States of America, and she did incredibly well at it.

First she moved to New York, setting herself up in a fancy apartment on Central Park West. She did what came naturally and collected for her natural talents.

Which was fine with her.

But, while New York liked her, she didn't much care for New York. It was too damned cold and damp, and since her trade was not the sort to limit one to a set location, there was little reason for her to remain in Manhattan if she didn't want to.

And she didn't.

She went first to Miami Beach, good territory for a good hustler. She earned good money and did what she wanted, working like a trouper, taking on all comers and doing anything they could possibly desire. She made a good living. When Miami Beach got tiresome she headed for Chicago, which got tiresome in an even shorter time. From Chicago she went to Phoenix, and then to Los Angeles, then San Francisco, then New Orleans, then somewhere else and somewhere else and somewhere else and somewhere else.

Doing the same thing everywhere she went.

Doing the same thing day after day, week after week, year after year.

It was her particular hobby and her particular business. She was good at it and she never ceased to enjoy it.

And, therefore, we may count her as one of the lucky ones. Her life may not strike us as an attractive one, but it was what she wanted and it made her happy. She earned her living on her back, earned a very good living on a very good back, and she enjoyed every damned minute of it. She never could get quite enough, not even when she was doing it for a living.

What more could she ask for?

What more could *anybody* ask for?

That brings us almost to the end. There are only two left, and they are the ones with whom we began. They are Walter and Mary Forsythe.

When Walt Forsythe finished his final telephone call he felt elated and disappointed at once. The disappointment resulted from the irritating fact that the group had run its course and dissolved. It had presented a tremendously diverting experience, and now it was over, and there would be no more amusement or entertainment forthcoming from weekly meetings. This, inevitably, was disappointing. Walt had enjoyed those meetings. It was something of a shame that they were over.

The elation stemmed from the fact that he had managed to outlive the group, that he was still going strong, that his old heart still pumped and his old brain still functioned. He was, in a sense, the winner—they had all left the ship, and he remained at the helm, strong and alive and free, a hard-eyed captain leading a battered ship through turbulent waters.

He went to Mary, told her about the phone calls, told her the group was disbanded.

"It's a shame," she said.

"It had to happen."

"I suppose so."

"It did," he said philosophically. "It ran its course and its course was over. Interesting while it lasted, but not permanent. Never permanent."

She agreed.

"It was good," he told her. "I enjoyed it, all of it. It was very good."

"It was good for me, too."

He grinned. "We're a couple of wild ones, Mary. We're no damned good. Evil people."

She smiled.

"Bad people," he said. "No damned good at all. When we die we'll go straight to hell."

"And shovel coal."

"Coal for the Devil," he said. "Better hell later on than hell on earth, that's the way I feel about it. I'll have my fun here and now. To hell with hell."

She smiled again. "What now?"

He looked up. "Now? Now I suppose I have to start thinking about a new group. Get some more people together. Have some more parties. See what develops."

"You're terrible, Walt."

"I know it. You're no angel yourself."

"No angel at all. You'll really get another party group going?"

"Of course."

"You're terrible, Walt."

He grinned.

"Come to bed," she said. "Come to bed with me and let's be terrible together."

He considered it.

"Please," she said. "I want you tonight. I want you very badly."

He thought about it, then shook his head. "I'm tired, Mary. And I've got thinking to do, thinking and planning and things."

"Scheming?"

"You could call it that."

"Scheming that's more important than taking good care of your wife?"

He grinned again. "I'm awfully tired," he said. "That's the real reason. You go to bed and I'll be in in a little while. Then we'll see what we can do."

She kissed him, turned and headed for the bedroom. He walked down the stairs slowly, found an easy chair and relaxed in it, his mind working.

Off they went again. Now he had to develop a group, a whole new group. He had to pick up a new set of friends, get a round of innocent parties going, drop the right sort of hints and notions until the climate was ripe for a game of Hide the Keys.

From there on it would be easy. The groundwork was the important part. There was nothing much to it after that was out of the way.

He sighed. A lot of work for a man who wasn't as young as he used to be, a man with a heart that couldn't last much longer. But it had lasted this far—lasted through many women and many hectic nights—lasted while the rest of them fell apart.

And it would go on lasting, until finally it ran out. And he knew how it would run out. He would die while he was making love to a woman, die in a woman's arms, and there could be no better way to go.

His mind buzzed with plans—people who were good prospects for a group, people to talk to, people to invite over for a few drinks. He thought of men he knew, men with wives he wanted, and he smiled a slow and evil smile.

He stayed in the chair for several hours, his mind buzzing with ideas, his heart ticking gently like a patient old clock. Then it was time to go to bed, and suddenly he wanted Mary very much, very much indeed, and he hurried up the stairs to her.

When he hit the very top step, Death took his heart in one massive fist and squeezed.

It is impossible to slate with assurance whether the

heart attack or the fall killed him. At any rate, the fall provided a perfect finishing touch. He tumbled end over end, and when he reached the bottom he reached it head first, and his head broke like an egg.

And, all at once, he was dead.

He had been wrong. It did not come in the arms of a woman. It came in the extremely simple act of ascending a staircase, came at once, with his old heart simply stopping of its own accord.

And he was dead.

MARY LIVED ON, BUT not for long. He was a bad man, and a sick man, but he was a lot of man, full and dynamic and intense, and Mary's life was one that depended upon having a man like Walt nearby.

Without him she was nothing. She went on in the house that was empty without him, took no lovers and lived no life, until she got sick and died.

No one went to the funeral.

SIXTEEN PEOPLE.

Larry Carson, an alcoholic, a bottle baby, damned by insecurity and inadequacy to the Bowery. A hopeless wreck, a wino, a wet brain, a hulk of a man with nothing inside, waiting for death.

Jackson Pierce, a man reborn, a success, happily married, happy to be alive.

Don and Nedra Marshall, free now, married, children, secure, happy. Almost dragged down but too strong to go under, back together after a struggle.

Joe and Roz Robshaw, another of the same with a harder fight behind them.

Peggy Phillips a lesbian, living in Greenwich Village and drifting from girl to girl, never staying too long, never living alone. A woman who lived with a man and bore his children, and who now lives with girls and bears no more children.

Bill Jansen, frightened, divorced from reality, afraid of failure, afraid of disappointing the world, self-emasculated, dead.

Pidge Jansen, living alone in a world very much her own, living in a world of hilarious rhymes and bitter laughter, dead yet still alive.

Steve Gordon, twice divorced, a bachelor again. playing the bachelor game. A success.

Nancy Gordon, divorced and divorced and divorced and divorced. Drifting from man to man to man to man looking for something she can never find.

Mark Phillips and Sue Carson. Mark and Sue Phillips now sharing their pain forever, living in a little house of hate.

Linda Pierce a prostitute.

Walt Forsythe, dead.

Mary Forsythe, dead.

THE WORLD GOES ON and the people in it go on living and loving, hating and dying. It is a tense and complex world and the people in it are tense and complex people. If you strain the world too much you will end it. If you drop enough bombs you will blow it to hell, and the world will split into pieces and be no more.

And the people are the same. If you hit them too hard they will crumble. If you tempt them too much they will fall. If you test them with tests that are too difficult they will fail these tests, and that will be the end of them. They will try, and they will fail, and that will be all there will be to it.

People are not good nor bad, not strong nor weak. People are complex souls, strong and weak at once, good and bad at once. They can be happy or they can be sad. They can win or they can lose. They can live or they can die.

But they must know themselves.

When they lose themselves in situations which are wrong for them, something must give. Either the situations must be changed or the people must change to conform to their new situations. This failing, the people crack under the strain.

There is a story about a man walking a long road. He was a tired man and the sun beat down upon him. The road stretched out, seemingly forever, but he had to follow it because the wilderness surrounded the road and he knew there was a town at the end of the road. A town meant food, a change of clothing, a bath, a good night's sleep. So he went on walking.

And, after many miles of traveling, he came to a fork in the road.

There was a signpost at the fork in the road. It told him that there was a town seven miles down each of the two prongs of the fork in the road. Neither town was any more attractive than the other.

The man was a perfectly logical and rational man. There was no reason for him to take the left fork rather than the right, no reason for him to take the right fork rather than the left.

He did not know which way to go. Because neither way was better than the other.

And so he went nowhere. He remained at the fork in the road, waiting for something to influence his decision, and eventually night came and he was still at the fork in the road.

He remained there.

And, when he finally decided the next morning that he had to go one way or the other, he tried to get up. But he was too weak.

So he stayed there, at the fork in the road, and died without food or water.

The man was incapable of choosing between two equal possibilities. It was a conflict which he could not solve, and it killed him.

Every man has a conflict he cannot solve. And, if he is forced to face it, it can kill him. Every man has a fork at which he must remain, a mirror into which he cannot bear to look, a secret place within himself which may remain forever closed to him.

MY NEWSLETTER: I get out an email newsletter at unpredictable intervals, but rarely more often than every other week. I'll be happy to add you to the distribution list. A blank email to lawbloc@gmail.com with "newsletter" in the subject line will get you on the list, and a click of the "Unsubscribe" link will get you off it, should you ultimately decide you're happier without it.

LAWRENCE BLOCK is a Mystery Writers of America Grand Master. His work over the past half century has earned him multiple Edgar Allan Poe and Shamus awards, the U.K. Diamond Dagger for lifetime achievement, and recognition in Germany, France, Taiwan, and Japan. His latest novel is *Dead Girl Blues*; other recent fiction includes *A Time to Scatter Stones*, *Keller's Fedora*, and *The Burglar in Short Order*. In addition to novels and short fiction, he has written episodic television (*Tilt!*) and the Wong Kar-wai film, *My Blueberry Nights*.

Block contributed a fiction column in Writer's Digest for fourteen years, and has published several books for writers, including the classic *Telling Lies for Fun & Profit* and the updated and expanded *Writing the Novel from Plot to Print to Pixel*. His nonfiction has been collected in *The Crime of Our Lives* (about mystery fiction) and *Hunting Buffalo with Bent Nails* (about everything else). Most recently, his collection of columns about stamp collecting, *Generally Speaking*, has found a substantial audience throughout and far beyond the philatelic community.

Lawrence Block has lately found a new career as an anthologist (*At Home in the Dark*; *From Sea to Stormy Sea*) and holds the position of writer-in-residence at South Carolina's Newberry College. He is a modest and humble fellow, although you would never guess as much from this biographical note.

Email: lawbloc@gmail.com
Twitter: @LawrenceBlock
Facebook: lawrence.block
Website: lawrenceblock.com